The Truth About Love

The Truth About Love

Josephine Hart

W F HOWES LTD

This large print edition published in 2009 by
W F Howes Ltd
Unit 4, Rearsby Business Park, Gaddesby Lane,
Rearsby, Leicester LE7 4YH

1 3 5 7 9 10 8 6 4 2

First published in the United Kingdom in 2009
by Virago Press

A CIP catalogue record for this book is available
from the British Library

ISBN 978 1 407 44155 9

Typeset by Palimpsest Book Production Limited,
Grangemouth, Stirlingshire
Printed and bound in Great Britain
by MPG Books Ltd, Bodmin, Cornwall

FSC
Mixed Sources
Product group from well-managed
forests and other controlled sources
Cert no. SGS-COC-2953
www.fsc.org
© 1996 Forest Stewardship Council

For my parents, brothers and sister . . .
in loving memory today and for always . . .

Often I've asked myself, but found no answer,
Where gentleness and goodness can possibly
  come from;
Even today I can't tell, and it's time to be
  gone.

Gottfried Benn, 'People Meet'

. . . and the sky rolled, rolling over me, heavy light. And bright too. Is it bright? Yes. And I lift my face to the light and I am flying towards it but I cannot reach it. And now I am falling, hurtling fast to the ground. And now the ground is close, closer, rushing hard. Please! Not yet! Please wait, ground. But the ground is now. And I am soft, me on so-hard ground. And I am all wet on such a dry day. And the wet is cold. I am cold-wet on a hot-dry day. And the sky rolls, rolls over me again. No birds, I can hear no birds. Were there birds before the sound? Can I make sound? Can I make words, sound? Can I see? What can I see? Is this dream-world? Are my eyes now the eyes of dream-world? No. It's not dream-world. I see something real in the real world. I see a bit of face, hers, sister-face, up close. An eye. Her eye. I see her eye for a second and my eye is hurt by what I see. Call out! Call out words! 'Get a priest and a doctor! Quickly! Quickly! Get a priest! Confession! Get priest first!' 'Bless me Father, for I have sinned.' 'How long?' he will ask. 'How long since last confession?' Last confession? Is this my last confession? No! Please. No. But I must make last confession to save my immortal soul. I remember first confession. Had no sins. Made them up. Told lies, at confession. Will I be able to tell my sins – my now-sins – now? Can anyone hear me? Sound? Am I making the sound for the words? My sister is bending over me. Close. 'Turn me over quickly! Don't let my mother see me! Mama mustn't see me like this.' Have the words come out? Look at sister-face. Can I hear anything? From her face? Must try to make my sister hear the sound of me. 'Turn me over quickly. Don't let Mama see me. Mama must not see.' And she hears me! I can see she hears me, above Mama's scream. Is it a scream? It's a sound. Sounds like a scream. Is it because my arm is gone? Can Mama see that my arm is gone? Yes! That's why sound is screaming. Mama must not see other parts gone as well. Gone where? Where is my arm gone? That sound again. Oh please don't Mama! That scream is hurting me. And now Olivia is pull-dragging Mama away. It's hard for Olivia because Mama is strong but Olivia holds on and pulls-drags Mama to the gate. Goodbye Mama. Can you hear me calling out? Goodbye kind Mama. Is it forever-goodbye?

And the sky rolls again. Rolling over me. And now I press into the ground. I hard press into the ground because the sky might roll me up into it and fly me away. Wait, sky! Olivia is running back to me now. She is here. I tell her 'arm is gone'. 'I know,' she says. 'I felt it fly away,' I say. And she says nothing. 'It's not only my arm,' I tell her. I don't tell her that

2

all down stomach-way feels strange. But maybe she sees. It feels like a nothing place. And my leg. Can I tell her about my leg? 'Gone – arm-side leg feels all soft. A leg shouldn't feel soft.' 'No,' she says, 'leg is all right.' 'No! No! It's not all right.' Am I fighting with my sister again? Want to call out to Mama, 'She won't listen to me Mama! She won't believe me.' But Mama isn't here to hear me.

Sky is rolling faster, helter-skelter. Suddenly. No warning, am sleepy. I am so sleepy. Then sister says 'Blanket!' Did she hear me think-say 'sleepy'? Then she says, 'For shock. Must get you a blanket for shock.' 'No,' I cry, 'don't go. Don't leave me! Please don't leave me, Olivia.' 'I must go.' She's determined. Mama often says 'she's very determined, your sister' and Mama smiles when she says that. 'I'll be back with blanket from bedroom. Back very quickly.' She is gone. Running. 'Don't fall! Don't fall!' I cry out to her. Does she hear me?

What's happened? Am I sick? No. I'm injured. No arm. Can't play rounders now. Was no good at hurling anyway. Now I see blood. I am injured. Yes. There's always blood when injured. Olivia's back with a sheet and a blanket and pillow. She's putting arm, part-arm on pillow. No hand. Hand gone. Gone from the elbow. And from my elbow something trails. White trail of something? What is it? She puts the sheet over my stomach and then the blanket. 'Have done it to myself this time, Olivia.' And she smiles – I used to call her Smiley-girl when I was small – and she cries at same time. 'Am not

3

drowning,' I say to her. 'You were always frightened I would drown even though I'm a great swimmer.' And she smiles again and cries again. But she makes no sound. No, I didn't drown. Not me. I remember lake-day when I dived deep down to show off to the girl over the road and everyone was frightened for me. Her name is Tara and she smiled at me when I came up through the water, shivering and a hero. I was so proud. 'Tara's very shy,' Mama says, 'and she's very petite.' And when I heard 'Reet Petite' on the wireless one day when they had all the old number-one hits I thought, she's my reet petite. Tara's my 'Reet Petite the finest girl you ever wanna meet.' I make everyone listen whenever it comes on. I love songs. I love lines of words. Line after line of them, like soldiers on the page. 'Stand up boys and sing the national anthem, "S-O-L-D-I-E-R-S are we, whose L-I-V-E-S are pledged to I-R-E-L-A-N-D."' Next line? What's next line? Stuff is falling away. Out of my mind. Where do thoughts fall when they fall out of your mind? On to hard ground and break into little pieces? Is my mind out of me? Mind on ground? Where is my brother?

'Where is Daragh?' I ask Olivia. 'We think he's still at the lake. Bogus Brogan and Mr Brannigan have gone to get him.' Her voice is talk-rolling over me. What is she saying now? Doctor coming? Good. Because pain is somewhere and it's coming for me. It's a little wriggly-saw pain. Pain-saw. Noisy. And big-noise pain further down the pain-shaft is coming for me. I can hear it. Fly me away from the pain

4

which is sawing me, pain – sawing louder and louder. And I'm going into some place of nothing at all only pain. Will anyone find me in pain-world? Or am I lost there? Can anyone save me? You can save the holy souls in purgatory years and years of pain if you pray for them, Brother Enda says. 'You can get them out with your prayers, boys. The power of prayer can release them from their pain-prison.' Jail-break? Love jail-break pictures. But I never said enough prayers for holy souls in purgatory. Now I have little second outside pain-world. Outside world! Am I going outside, world? No! I want the world. I want to stay in the world. Even pain-world.

Hear front gate banging now. 'You must do something about the banging of that gate, Tom.' Mama's been saying that for months. Hear running. Someone is near and here now. A doctor! Know by his bag. That's a great bag. But he's not my known-doctor. Name? What is name of known-doctor? Dr Sullivan! Now black-white man is talking to me. 'Son? Son?' But he's not my father. 'Dada? Can't see Dada.' 'Dada is not here yet,' says Olivia. Father Dwyer! It's Father Dwyer beside me. He is kneeling, black-white, beside me. 'Don't let your mother hear you, son.' Can she hear me still? She's in the front, isn't she? But perhaps am making too-sad sound? Must try to be a hero, not a cry-baby. 'Be a soldier now, son.' But am not a soldier and am not his son either. Will never be a soldier. Will Father Dwyer whisper *'Te absolvo'*? Will he whisper *'Te absolvo'* so that all secret sins will be forgiven? Will he want

5

a list? But the others will hear! Olivia will hear! But if I don't give a list all sins will not be forgiven. He hasn't whispered 'If thou livest' so I'm in the world still. Bend low, Father, and I'll whisper my sins. I don't want to meet Word-Man-God with secret sin still on my soul. But now Father Dwyer is shaking his head. Don't do that! I'm frightened.

Doctor holding needle. Injection now. See it. Feel it. I never cried when I had injections. Ever. Daragh used to cry at everything when he was small. Said it was best because then you got sweets. Injection is in me. And now remember injection-doctor's name. Carter! Protestant! Telling me 'Good boy, good boy.' And am hero on stretcher being carried out. Feel am floating up into rolling sky where the doctor is hiding the pain, and where maybe Father Dwyer has hidden my secret sins of impure thoughts and deeds, all hidden-forgiven on sky-rolling day. Am going through garage now, past garden. Olivia is standing at the edge of the lawn between crying-kneeling Mama and me. Her head quick-turning to me then to Mama. To me. To me or to Mama? Her hair swings, her head swings, swings high-low in the sudden breeze. She is not certain which way to turn. Which way to stay turned? Which way to stay turned away? From me? Or away from Mama? 'Oh Mama' I hear floating crying sound from Olivia. And for just a sight-second I see her again, Mama. My Mama, in the front garden. Rocking forwards and back-wards. Dancing! Not dancing. Rocking. Forwards.

Backwards. Rock-rolling. Head down. Head back. Rock, rock, 'we're gonna rock around the clock tonight'. Round the clock on train of thought. Fast train. Going faster. Faster on train of thought. Can say nothing. Past sound-stations, hurtling.

Now going out the gate, and sister? She is staying with rocking Mama. Then I hear her call out 'Dada! Dada!' He's here! Is Dada here? Yes! I see him. Oh Dada! Oh! But Dada's quick-running towards rocking-Mama, towards crying-kneeling-rocking-Mama. 'See you later alligator/ After 'while crocodile/ Can't you see you're in my way now?/ Don't you know you cramp my style?' I cannot see him now. No.

And now am through banging gate. Just see corner of Mrs Garvey's house as they hurry-carry-rock me into ambulance, white-white ambulance. 'Rock-a-bye baby in the tree top, when the wind blows the cradle will rock.' Next line? 'When the bough breaks, the cradle will fall.' Baby falling. Mrs Garvey drops her babies before they're ready. 'Summer must be a bad time for me, Mrs O'Hara,' I heard her say to Mama. 'I feel guilty, as though I'd dropped them carelessly and spilled them, like milk out of a churn onto the dirty lane. That's the fourth baby I've lost.' Mama didn't drop me too fast. She held on to me. Didn't drop me too soon. But Mama, I think I'm falling now and you can't catch me. 'Rock-a-bye baby.' The ambulance is moving. Stop! Let me back! Let me go home. Please. Please. Or even let me into Mrs Garvey's house. I was there today, in her

7

dark little back room. She was sitting there by herself, said she wanted to hide her crying face from the light. And she told me something that I was dying to tell Mama. What was it? She was crying when she told me. I asked her, should I put on the wireless to cheer her up? 'Yes,' she said, 'you do that, lad.' 'Irene goodnight, Irene goodnight . . . Goodnight Irene, goodnight Irene. I'll see you in my dreams . . . Last Saturday night I got married . . .' 'Oh Mrs Garvey! That's my mother's favourite golden oldie! She loves that song. She's always singing it. Mama has a grand voice.' 'I know, lad.' And we listened to it all the way through and then I had to go home. 'I'm dying to tell my mother, Mrs Garvey.' What was it I was dying to tell my mother?

We're turning now. We must be in Mount Road; soon we'll be past the school. School passed. Passed my exams. Specially science with Brother Rory and history and English with Brother Enda. Moving fast now. Very fast now. I remember the day everyone was cross with me because I roller-skated down the Bridge Road so fast. Faster, faster down the road and I nearly went slide-falling under a car and hurt my elbow badly. Pain awful but was laughing anyway. Laughing. Dr Carter is looking close at me. He's not smiling. And I hear shouting from the front . . .

'For Christ's sake, Billy. Slow down. Not so fast!'
He's using the Lord's name in vain.
'Behold Saint Christopher – then go thy way in safety.'

'He wasn't talking of seventy-miles-an-hour, Billy.'

'The Man understands.'

'Dr Carter?'

'He's going. We'll lose him if we don't get there quickly.'

'Jesus that was close!'

He's taken the Lord's name in vain. Again. Venial sin. Confession on Friday? Friday! So far away, Friday, from today, Thursday. Thursday's child has far to go.

'Mind out for that child! For Christ's sake who lets a four-year-old out of their sight?'

'It's the McLoughlin child. Those McLoughlins! They're drowning in children. Makes them careless.'

Careless? With babies? So many ways to lose a baby. Even born babies. I'm not a baby. I'm not a child. I'm a lad. A going-away lad. Oh Mama, Mama.

'Oh God Almighty the lad's crying for his mother. I can't bear that sound.'

Has he heard it before? Let me out of the ambulance. I'm not ready for eternity. Not yet! Not yet! I've got something I'm dying to tell my mother. If Mrs Garvey ever has a son she'll name him after me. Yes! Mama? Did you hear that, Mama?

'Oh God! Listen to him. He's groaning. Watch out! Watch out for the fucking lorry! Watch out, Billy!'

They're swearing! They're saying 'fuck'. Who's swearing? 'Not me Mama. I promise.' If only they wouldn't shout . . .

9

'Is he conscious?'

Yes. Yes, I am . . . Yes.

'What'll I ever say to Tom O'Hara? He's a lovely man.'

Everybody says that. 'Your father's a lovely man.'

'Tom O'Hara's a brave man too. Always trying to calm that mad neighbour of his, Jim Brannigan, and his terrible rages against Marjorie and the two little boys. She's always running to Tom to save them. The lad's bravery didn't come from nowhere.'

Dada! Dada! Dada! *De profundis clamavi ad te/ Domine, Domine* . . . Out of the depths to Thee, oh Lord, I cry. Dada, Dada, I call to thee, Dada, Dada. I call to thee. From the depths. From the depths. I'm falling and calling to thee. Don't let me fall, Dada! Am not falling from the roof, Dada! Am falling from life, Dada! Am falling from life. Into eternity, Dada. Forever and ever amen. Am so very frightened of the loneliness, Dada.

'I saw worse wounds in the war. Some survived.'

The war? They say Dr Carter was a Major. On the English side. Dr Sullivan is our doctor. He's in Tipperary today with 'that hopeless son' of his. Heard that at the lake – was it today? When I met the German on his walk and I told him I loved his gate, his hero-gate. I've wanted to tell him before but I was a bit shy. 'I love your gate, Mr Middlehoff. It's a hero's gate.' 'What is it that makes you say that?' He pronounces every word like he loves the English language but he's afraid of it. 'The helmet on top.' 'Ah,' he said.

'And who is your hero?' 'Sarsfield is my hero. Olivia prefers Pearse. She worships him. She knows every word of his "Boys of Ireland" speech but so do I, but . . .' 'Are you one of the boys of Ireland?' he asked me. '"*Mise Éire*. I am Ireland." Ireland is me.' 'And what else are you?' 'Nothing else. I try to live up to that precept, as Brother Enda calls it. Purity in heart and soul for Ireland. Goodbye, Mr Middlehoff, I have to go to the boat now. I hope I'll see you on your walk tomorrow.' But I won't. Not now. He's nice to me. He's nicer than Mr Pennington who used to own Lake House. The German's more like Mrs Garvey, a grown-up who listens to me. Who will listen to me now? What's happening now? We're slowing down.

'Thank God! We're through the gates. There's Father Dwyer's car!'

I don't think Father Dwyer heard my confession properly. Am I in a state of sin? Think. Think. Secret sin. Oh, I'm so ashamed of secret sin. 'Bless me Father,' I try so hard not to commit secret sin. When it all comes over me I can't stop. 'Bless me father for I have sinned.' Oh bless me. So hard to tell that other sin when I stroked the hair of across-the-road girl. Name? I had her name! Where has my mind gone for a name? Tara! 'Reet Petite.' Mama says you're petite. I'm so sorry Mama, so sorry. You'll be thinking of me. And crying all the time. Again. You're not well, Mama. It was too hard on you, everyone

11

said that last year when you cried and cried all the time. I used to go off to my room and hide in a corner when you cried so long last year after little sister died. And we all knelt and looked and looked that day at her as she lay white in her white communion dress and you wouldn't leave the room would you Mama? Dr Sullivan and Dada and Father Dwyer had to talk you out of the room. It took hours and hours. We sat outside waiting for you, Olivia, Daragh and me. And then after the funeral in the rain and cold we all came home and the house was full. And then it was quiet. And then it was Christmas and I got a book. Was that my last Christmas?

'God, the hospital's drenched in sunshine. It's dripping in it. What a day. Like they said on Radio Eireann this morning, "Days like this don't come in twos." What have I said? Don't die on us all now, lad. Lad, can you hear me? Don't die on us all! Though maybe it's better. He's destroyed, isn't he? There's Matron. Oh thank God she's here. She's one great woman with that starched head-dress of hers and the rustling skirts. I'm surprised death ever defies her. I'm surprised she doesn't bully death out of every bed in this hospital or laugh it out.'

Laugh death out of bed? Can I laugh it away? Can I laugh and be like the great hero of old Cúchulainn? who cried, 'If I die it shall be from the excess of love I bear the Gael.' Ah, what a line! I've left no lines behind me. If I die I'll have

12

died silent. Nothing to be remembered by. I could have written something. A poem, even. Even one poem. Go away. Death! I'll try laughing it away, like Cúchulainn. But now I feel a kind of rolling again and the woman is talking, the white and dark-blue woman.

'Oh my God! Childie! Dr Sullivan and I delivered you. Ah childie, what have you done to yourself? Come here to me, childie. Darling lad, I helped your mother Sissy bring you into this world. Oh Sissy, what can we ever do for you now? All right everyone! Now up the steps. Right. Let's get down to theatre. They're waiting for him. It'll be a long night what-ever happens. Pray. All of you pray that Mr Connelly – the best surgeon in the county – does the will of God tonight. The lad may be better off if God takes him. God will decide. But we'll do our best. Hurry now. Hurry . . .'

Hurry! Run a race down the corridor. Down. Am going down life corridor. Into theatre. What play am I in? Real life. It's real life! What is real life? Reen. Irene goodnight Irene . . . Reet Petite . . . Irene goodnight Irene. Reet reen reet . . . the finest girl you ever wanna meet . . . I go to meet my maker. Not yet! Mama, Dada, where are you? Where? Last hours, like Pearse. Alone. But I have no last poem for you, Mama. Not like his for his mother before the British shot him. We all had to learn it. Olivia used to make visitors cry when she recited 'The Mother': 'I do not grudge them: Lord, I do not

13

grudge/ My two strong sons that I have seen go out/ To break their strength and die . . .' Pale Pearse, pale like me, she says. Tried to be a hero to Mama. 'Turn me over, don't let my mother see me.' Not much of a hero. No one will tell my story. Oh Mama, I feel all wet and cold . . . I can hear you Mama: 'Come in child. Out of the rain. You'll get drenched. Come over here by the fire, I'll hotten you up.' You always said that Mama. Oh thank you Mama for hot drinks on cold nights, for long-sitting through gasping asthma, for looking away from down there when you helped me out of the bath because I was very weak once. Mama, Dada, am off to Tír na nÓg. I'm sorry, but I think I will have to go there now. There's nowhere else for me. I can't stay here. Goodnight Mama. The land of Tír na nÓg, the land of the young is bundling up the clouds, high, high. Am sky-flying. Hold on to me, Mama! Hold on! Don't let me fly away! Hold on to me! Catch my legs! Leg! Other one too soft. Bone soft. Something's wrong. Hold on to my good leg. Hold on Mama! Mama? Dada! Hold on! You're heavier, Dada. Heavier than Mama. So you hold on to me, Dada. Don't let go of me Dada. Dada? Irene goodnight Irene. Ireeeeeene goodnight . . . Goodnight Mama Irene good-night, I'll see you in my dreams. Dreams. Dreams. Goodnight . . . goodnight. Oh Ireeene goodnight Irene. Ireeeeene goodnight . . . good-night Mama . . . Irene goodnight I'll see you in

14

my dreams. It takes some time to fall asleep. I'll see you there. Hold my leg Dada! Am floating all away. Dream dreaming. I dream of you. Irene goodnight Ireeeene, goodnight . . . goodnight Ireene . . . I'll see you in my dreams.

'Dada?'

'Olivia? Is that you, Olivia?'

'It is Dada. I'm here outside your bedroom door.'

'Come in child.'

'No, Dada. I'm standing outside. Can you come out Dada?'

'Ah! Ah! Yes. Coming, child.'

'What is it, Tom? Tom, what is it? What's happening? Olivia? Olivia! Come in here this minute.'

'No Mama. It's nothing Mama, it's nothing. Just there's a mouse in my room. Will you come Dada? Will you come now? Quickly!'

'Coming, child. I'm coming.'

'That's rubbish, Olivia. Go back to sleep. You're seventeen. Tell her, Tom. Tell her she's got to stop this nonsense about mice and spiders in her room. It's all nonsense.'

'Ah please Mama, if Dada'd just come and check for me I can go back to sleep and we can all go to see him in the hospital first thing in the morning. Please come now Dada.'

'I'm coming, child.'

'Don't close the door Tom!'

'I think I will Sissy. You need to sleep, Sissy. I'll be back in a minute. And don't worry, she'll grow out of the spider thing.'

'She's seventeen Tom . . . ah . . . Hurry back to me Tom.'

'I will Sissy. I will. I'll just close the door for a second.'

'Olivia? Child?'

'He's dead.'

'Oh my God. Oh my God. Who told you?'

'Father Dwyer. Just now. I heard a car turn into the road. I knew it must be Dr Carter or Father Dwyer. I knew he was dead. About half an hour ago. I just knew. I felt it. I felt him . . . gone. I got up and I dressed and sat on my bed. And I waited. For the news. And it came. I heard the gate and then I opened the door – I didn't want him to press the bell – and Father Dwyer was just standing there. I looked at him and he shook his head. He couldn't find the words. And I closed the door on him. And I went into my room and thought, how can I bring the news to Dada without her knowing first? And I thought of all my old fears – spiders and mice . . . ah Dada, Dada. What will we find to help us tell her? What words will we find? Where will we find them?'

'I don't know, Olivia. I really thought we'd have time. I thought this awful night – hiding the truth

17

from her – lying there – a liar – trying to save her from the truth, clawing at time, Olivia – we clawed at time to try to save her from the shock – to get her through the shock – which I thought would kill her. I was certain it would kill her and that if we could hold it off – then I'd give the time to him. I thought he had a chance. I thought he'll be unconscious and . . . They'll come to tell me – to come – they'll tell me – I was waiting for Sullivan . . . What have I done? Oh God, what have I done? God must help me now. Help our family. Help us tell her. We'd better face it now Olivia. There is no waiting now. No way out of this one, is there Olivia? Listen child, whatever you're about to see – after all you've seen today – know it can be survived. Just stay beside me, Olivia, and together we'll go to the bedroom. Just wait for a second. Help me now God, because now I'm going to open that door slowly.'

'Tom? Tom?'

'Yes. Yes, Sissy. Darling, Sissy.'

'Did you find the mouse?'

'No Sissy. You were right. There was no mouse.'

'There's never been a mouse! Have you ever found a mouse or a spider in that girl's bedroom?'

'No, Sissy.'

'What were you two whispering out there in the dark? What Tom? What whispering? What?'

'I think we must face it now Olivia. Hold my hand now, Olivia. We can't stop her knowing now. It's rolling in, rolling over us, the truth.'

18

'Olivia was always too imaginative wasn't she, Tom?'

'Say nothing now, Olivia.'

'Wasn't she, Tom, always too imaginative? And tonight, how could she do that to us tonight? Too imaginative. Tom? Olivia? Answer me! Weren't you always too imaginative? Wasn't she, Tom? Put on the light Tom! Tom? Let me look at you Tom. In the light. Come over to me. Look at me in the light.'

'Here I am Sissy.'

'Come closer Tom. Let me look at you Tom, in the light.'

'Look at me Sissy. Look at me.'

'Oh no! No! No! No and no.'

'Oh my God Olivia . . . Stop it, Sissy. Stop beating your fists on the wall, Sissy you'll hurt yourself. Let me hold you, darling Sissy.'

'No, no. Not my boy. Not my darling boy. Not my darling child, my darling boy . . .'

'Stop it Mama.'

'Olivia, run to Daragh's room. Don't let him in here.'

'Let me beat this wall for him. Let me out of this bed. I will beat the floor down to the earth . . . Let me beat down the earth for him, my darling boy. Boy. Boy. Never let me stop beating this down, beating it down.'

'Hurry – stop Daragh, Olivia. Go now.'

'I'll be back in a second Dada.'

'Ah Sissy, let me hold you Sissy.'

'Let go of me Tom. Let me beat this down, down.'

'Olivia?'

'It's all right Dada. Daragh's just sitting there looking out the window. He's not even crying. What's that noise at the door? Someone's beating on the front door. Why don't they ring the bell? Ah there! The bell's ringing. I'll get it Dada.'

'Dr Sullivan! Come in.'

'Where is she, Olivia? Where's your mother?'

'They're in the bedroom.'

'Right. Let's go. Tom? Ah Tom, what can I say? Stop that, Sissy! Give me your arm. Come on now. You've got to do this for me. Sissy I want you to stay still for just a second. I'm going to give you an injection. Help me roll up the sleeve of her nightdress, Tom. This will knock her out. She won't sleep for that long but when she wakes she will be under control. Good girl, Sissy. Let's get you back into bed. Well done. God, why wasn't I here when it happened? I know why! Christ, I was in Tipperary with that bloody son of mine who is never out of . . . Oh God, sorry Tom, me talking about my boy. Sorry. I got here as fast as I could. I talked to Carter and to the surgeon, Connelly. There never was any hope at all. No hope at all that he could have survived what happened. And Tom it's best that he didn't. Hold on to that piece of knowledge. And here take these. These pills will take the edge off the shock of it. I'll give half a one each to Olivia and Daragh. Do what you're told now, Tom. And Tom, I know why you did what you did – staying here with Sissy. In holding it off – the truth, by staying with her here, keeping her away from the hospital – you did the right thing to try to pretend for a few hours. She's been so ill after the death of the little girl. So you bought her a few hours. Essential Tom, because with the raw memory of the other, this shock would have been too much for her. Her mind needed time to absorb it a bit. I'd say she knew immediately but she ran to a hidden place, a buried place. And you gave her time there Tom. You saved her mind. You saved Sissy. And that's love, Tom. Love helped you do the right thing. You were right. Remember that. No man has ever loved a woman more.'

'Love? For love we're asked to do the strangest things in life. Love! It asks the strangest sacrifices.'

CHAPTER 1

. . . today, June 18th 1962, I, Thomas Middlehoff, known locally as 'the German', attend my first Irish funeral. My housekeeper Bridget informed me that there would be no objection. The iconography of this particular death and burial is an unfamiliar one in this place that has known peace for decades. As in all such towns there are recognised routes to eternity: the heart that fails; the cells that in either boredom or rebellion rise up against their host and triumph; the accidental tumble over the edge of life in cars or on bicycles; the exhausted surrender to the sudden storm on water, which 'tossed the boat around like . . .' – the metaphor is always dramatic. All these routes eventually seem to have been pre-ordained. This one does not.

The intensity of heat that yesterday had so star-tled this small town in Ireland has today abated somewhat. The sun shines but its light is now less troubling. The day is warm but it no longer soars in triumph as though it had wished to teach an uncomfortable lesson to those who had failed to factor its burning rays into their sartorial decisions.

The cathedral is full. Mourners who'd arrived

too late to be seated huddle in the aisles, some leaning against the confessional boxes in which they normally kneel in darkness. I stand at the back and carefully follow the proceedings in a missal loaned to me by Bridget. It had been handed to me with an air of solemnity, as though it were an ancient letter of introduction that would guarantee safe passage to its recipient. Bridget herself had received it from her grandmother, no doubt with equal solemnity. Bridget has two missals. The new one, a gift from her son, has, perhaps due to a generational imperative, supplanted in importance the older gift which, nevertheless, I was honour-bound to return to her after the funeral.

The ritual of mass begins with the sign of the cross, the ultimate emblem of the sacrifice that mass celebrates. So that no one need doubt its significance, the sign of the cross is made no fewer than fifty-two times during the ceremony. Bridget's son had evidently counted them once at a Sunday mass, a fact that, though it impressed Bridget greatly, implied to me that this was not a boy in whom resided excessive reverence.

This is a Mass for the dead. Bridget has explained to me that as such it is shorter, due to the omission of certain psalms, 'Judica me', which Bridget had quoted to me with such feeling I had later turned to it in the missal and memorised it. 'For Thou art my strength; Why hast Thou cast me off? And why do I go sorrowful whilst the enemy afflicteth me?' It is magnificent. Its omission is appropriate.

I concentrate on my missal and after some time I note a certain stirring in the congregation. Slowly the mourners stand up and move from their pews. Someone behind me whispers 'offerings'. An orderly queue is formed and men – mostly, I would guess from their age and bearing, the heads of families – are joined by a number of women who shuffle forward with lowered faces, clutching large handbags to them as though they were an aid to gender identification. A number of the men hold white envelopes clasped tightly in their hands and stare straight ahead. Others have placed their envelope carefully in a jacket pocket from which it slightly protrudes, like the edge of a carefully ironed handkerchief.

'All move forward silently until they stand before Tom O'Hara and Father Dwyer who are positioned together behind a dark carved-wood table. This has been placed to the left of a small side chapel, in which, on a high bier, the body of Tom O'Hara's son lies in its coffin. Each man hands over his envelope, his offering. I note all this as I too make my way forward, as Bridget had told me would be expected of me. When it is finally my turn to stand before this man, this bereaved father, Tom O'Hara, I do not look at him. I had noted from their bowed heads that those in front of me had also failed this test of courage. His 'thank you' is muffled. It's a strange gratitude. Bridget had informed me that all monies go to the Parish and that the amount collected is, in a sense, a measure of the sympathy and grief. Measure for measure. As I walk back to my pew I observe Mrs O'Hara and her daughter and son sitting in the front pew. They sit motionless, isolated in a place of honour no one begrudges them.

Then it is over. Everyone stands. Family and relatives now make their way to the side chapel. To bear witness, no doubt, as the coffin is borne out to the waiting hearse on the shoulders of men, among them his father. Mourners scatter; the men scurry, heads down, towards their cars. Their wives walk slowly, smartly dressed, suits mostly though it is a summer day, heads adorned with discreet hats, mantillas on the heads of the younger women. Car doors open and close with care. Noise cannot be borne today. Everyone, even children, sense the need for quietness.

I decide that I too will walk behind the hearse. It is, I feel, correct that I should do so. It is appropriate. And so the long, slow procession trails its way through the town in which today, for this cortège, every shop has closed. Had it been a state funeral it could not have been more evocative of a dignified expression of grief. At last, perhaps after forty minutes, we arrive at the graveyard, one of mankind's most underrated symbols of civilisation. A small graveyard is a most particular resting place. It is a place in which the dead may nestle but do not mingle. Here, in this Irish cemetery, the mass grave is unknown. A certain propriety maintains.

As the coffin of the boy is lowered there is a

dangerous moment. The boy's sister seems to sway forwards toward the open grave. In a second she is caught. A priest places his hands, with some force, on her shoulders and steadies her. Separation of the dead from the living often requires strength. Another continues with the prayers.

A handful of earth is thrown over the coffin and the process of filling in a grave commences. After some time mourners begin to drift away. I look around awkwardly, aware that Dr Carter is in conversation with Father Dwyer and that Bishop Fullerton is speaking quietly to Mr O'Hara. I am an observer and a stranger, the one I feel almost essential to the other. The elective outsider, the truthful observer of the scene requires an anatomical eye, which I have endeavoured over the years to develop.

My eye now meets that of another, it is caught and trapped for a moment by that of Mrs O'Hara. There is no escape from it. Her eye is a cold eye, unblinking, frozen perhaps in a memory of what it has witnessed. I take a step toward her but she turns away. I am released into freefall. Then the vision comes unbidden. Why does the mind allow intrusion against our will? I saw her falling. I saw my mother falling. She did not fall in parts. She fell in her entirety through a powder of the dove-grey dust of shattered masonry. The white-grey stone leg of the statue of a tall young man fell with her. The subtle difference in the shades of white and grey that day delineated contours as sharply as crimson on a black background. The stone boy had stood

26

sentinel in the long colonnade that connected the drawing room to the conservatory. He had been a reliable companion in the childhood games I had played with my brother. He had been just. He had never taken sides. The conservatory, I remember, did not disintegrate that day. Such anomalies are more common in the aftermath of bombing than one might imagine. My mother had just left the drawing room and was, in her last minutes, close to her stone companion who, heroically, fell with her, his leg the first dismembering, then the second, his arm. It broke off in an arc and for a moment it seemed as though he threw it towards her – as if to say, 'Take it, take it! Cling to this, this part of me that I offer to you.' Then the falling, fast. The vision dies. And I am here, again, in this place. At an Irish funeral, my first Irish funeral.

Bishop Fullerton now approaches Mrs O'Hara. He talks to her. Rather, he talks at her. She simply looks at him. Does he also feel trapped? He steps back from her slightly. I move forwards. Each of us is wrong. She turns away and toward her husband. It's time to go home. Tom O'Hara guides her away. Mourners separate to make a path for them. Priest and bishop stand aside for them. Their grief takes precedence over the normal hierarchical structure of this community. Murmuring quietly, a procession follows them. Some scatter to left or right to stand by other graves. Eamonn, the bishop's driver, who takes him to and from my house for our chess evenings, approaches me.

Would I like to go with the bishop to the O'Hara's house? I am uncertain whether this invitation comes from Bishop Fullerton or from the O'Hara family. I decline. I will walk home. Though hours remain this day is over.

CHAPTER 2

It is not true that I discourage visitors from Lake House. It is, however, true that I do not issue invitations. I exclude from this assessment my monthly chess game with Robert Carter and, on separate evenings, with Bishop Fullerton. Since this is a surprisingly formal society I am untroubled by any intrusion by townspeople, other than those who make the three-mile journey for the not necessarily companionable purpose of earning their living.

There exists between myself and Bridget, my non-resident housekeeper, respect, tolerance, and on her part determination that Irish charm will eventually wear me down and I will, 'like all strangers who come here, Mr Middlehoff, fall in love with the place'. Her use of my name is in its own way an act of intimacy, since I am aware that in the town they simply call me 'the German'. As a statement of exclusion this is as accurate as it is definitive. It is one I welcome. I believe I carry with me what every German carries with them, an aura, an emanation. I am German. You know me. I regard myself as under an obligation in this matter. 'That this is done shall stand for ever more.' And a day. I am mindful of my responsibility as a member of a cursed tribe. In Ireland there is of course no '*te absolvo*'. There is, however, little interest in a story of evil that the Irish do not fully believe possible. For had they known the truth, some slight readjustment to their view of their own modern history might have been necessary. The moral demands, even of peripheral images, might have blurred the purity of their ancient vision. However, I continue to appreciate a certain discretion concerning the history of my country that I had not found elsewhere in my exile.

Though I remain sensible to my inclusion almost two months ago in the congregation of mourners at the funeral of the boy, I do not seek, nor have I been offered, further integration. Robert Carter, whose medical attendance on the day of the accident had been in a sense accidental, has also retreated to the comparatively isolated position of Protestant doctor in an Irish town. My friendship with him, a former Major in the Medical Corps of the British Army, is no doubt mysterious to them. Perhaps they are convinced that it is based solely on a passion for the game of chess, a game for which their temperament renders them wholly unsuited. As I wondered whether my father would agree with this judgement I hear the sound of a car on gravel and, looking from my study window, see Tom O'Hara emerge from his battered Morris

Minor like a man who had been trapped too long in a small cupboard and must now carefully test the limbs that had been forced into abnormal contortions. He looks around and then, it seems, straight at me as I stand by the window. I have no alternative but to leave my study and proceed down the long parquet-floored hall towards the dark oak door that separates me from this uninvited guest. I open my heavy door, slowly.

'Good morning Mr Middlehoff. I've come about the gate.'

'Good morning Mr O'Hara.'

'Good morning Mr Middlehoff,' he says again. And again, 'I've come about the gate.'

The note is abrupt, even peremptory. How am I to respond? This man, whose rather leonine head and large body speak to a slower, calmer nature, is now in a place I recognise and I know the price the terrain exacts. Courtesy, absolute courtesy is now required. It is a balm and today I apply it for my own protection as well as his.

'Which gate, Mr O'Hara? Which gate? I'm sorry, Mr Mr O'Hara but I do not know to what you refer.'

'Didn't your estate manager, Tim, mention it?'

'No.'

'I asked him to. You're sure he didn't mention it?'

'I am sure.'

'Well then I'm sorry. I wouldn't be here otherwise.'

'No?'

'Do you think I would just turn up at a stranger's house, Mr Middlehoff? Just turn up here and ask him for a gate? Is that what you think of us? Is that the kind of people you think we are?'

'I'm sorry, Mr O'Hara. This a surprising visit and a most surprising request. As for Tim, he is spending a week in Wexford.'

'In Wexford?'

'Yes.'

'Must be the sister then.'

'Yes.'

'Well, well! The gate. The one with the helmet on the top. You know the one: it marks the end of Lake Lane. You brought it here. Took down Edmund Pennington's old wooden gate.'

'I know the gate, Mr O'Hara. It marks the perimeter of my land. So indeed I know the gate.'

'Of course you do. It's yours! Well, I want to buy it from you.'

'You wish to purchase my gate from me? Why?'

'My son, the lad, admired it. Saw it all the time when he waited in the club rowing boat for the island swimmers to be ready. Gazed at it, told me he made up stories about it. Said it was a warrior's gate because of the carved helmet at the top. He was at that age. Warriors, heroes, you know.'

And I remember my last conversation with the boy.

'I know what you mean and may I again, Mr O'Hara, express my deepest sympathy to you and your family.'

32

'Thank you. Thank you. I'm aware it's a very strange request.'

'It is, Mr O'Hara.'

'I've got it in my head no other gate will do.'

'That is something that often happens. Will you please come in, Mr O'Hara? Coffee, perhaps?'

'Coffee? No, but thank you. We're not great coffee drinkers here. We don't want stimulants, you see. We want oblivion.'

They all talk like this. It's their gift, their armour. Now he begins to pace around my courtyard.

'Do you mind if I just stay outside? Keep walking? It helps me.'

'Not at all.'

It's a common reaction *in extremis*. Mostly people walk in circles. They know there is no escape. As if he reads my thoughts he says, 'Walking helps me . . . movement without escape. Sissy, my wife, wants to escape. I don't think there's anywhere to escape to. Leaving the place won't work.'

'Ireland is full of towns like this, no?'

'No. Not for us, Mr Middlehoff.'

'I see.'

'Let me ask you, Mr Middlehoff, did it work for you? Leaving the place?'

'I don't know yet.'

'Well I don't trust the idea. Living close to what is lost, that's the only way.'

'Living close to what is lost? I will remember that, Mr O'Hara.'

'Isn't it too late? For you?'

There it is! The sudden, assumed intimacy. So quick. So unexpected. I have noted this characteristic before in conversations with them. Close, closer. Then the essential distancing. For protection?

'In what way?'

'You left the place.'

'True. But you will not?'

'No. We will not.'

'How does your wife feel about that?'

'How does Sissy feel?'

'Yes, how does Mrs O'Hara feel about your decision?'

'It's early days. But I think she's resigned.'

'Resignation! Ah.'

'We learn it early here. God's will.'

'Resignation, even without the comforts of religion, can be very important.'

'Our religion is not always that comforting.'

'Is Mrs O'Hara resigned?'

'To staying here?'

'To everything.'

'It's her only hope, Mr Middlehoff. Resignation is her only hope.'

'Hope in resignation? I will remember, that Mr O'Hara.'

'Well now, Mr Middlehoff, you seem to be paying a lot of attention to my words. Thank you. You're a most courteous man. I appreciate it. But what I really want is to buy your gate from you.

34

If that sounds rude, I'm sorry. I'm a bit raw at the moment.'

'I do not consider you at all rude. But I do need to consider your request.'

I do not wish to say no immediately. He is indeed too raw.

'You are certain you will stay here? That if I give it to you it will stay with you?'

I lie, of course, in this false pursuit of truth. Kindness? Perhaps.

'Yes. We'll stay. And don't think I didn't try to help Sissy in her sudden search for escape to another place. I played fair though I knew she was wrong. I always knew there was no escape from what we have to suffer. I'm not certain anyone here understands exactly what we have been through. The violence of it, you see . . .'

'Yes.'

'I've taken her to half the towns in the Province of Leinster. Didn't take long – there aren't that many of them. We went on little drives, just looking you know, in the evening or on a Sunday. We even went to the city of Dublin – where I was born.'

'I did not know that.'

'Why should you? Anyway, after Dublin, which held too much noise for her and too many noisy memories for me, we tried Tullamore, where she was young once. But as I guessed it would, it reminded her too much of her youth and what was lost. Not youth but everything since youth. Then we went one day all the way down to

Tipperary – longer drive, that one. She knew no one in Tipperary and neither did I. Well, I suppose Dr Sullivan's son, but that's another story. We looked at houses from the outside, you know just looking and getting the feel of the place. I'd point out the advantages of each spot. Like I said, I was fair. She was beside me in the front, the other two, Olivia and Daragh, sitting in the back, saying nothing. The whole business was silent apart from, 'Look at that one Sissy!' Or, 'What do you think of Tipperary?' No response, of course. But what was there to say? There was some idea in her mind that a new place would change, if not everything, then at least something. Help with the memories. That the newness of a scene would make memory fade. But whatever road we drove down it was following behind. Whatever house we looked at along the way – just from the outside they all seemed to be empty. Empty of our lives, which, in the end, was all we had.'

'I understand.'

'And Sissy, you see Sissy is so tired. She's beyond tired, to tell you the truth. Too much loss. She's in some place where I can't find the old Sissy.'

'After a tragedy, many survivors are lost.'

'Say that again.'

'After a tragedy, many survivors are lost.'

'Well now you've given me a thought there.'

'A balance perhaps, Mr O'Hara. After all you gave me living close to what is lost.'

36

'That's how we exist here: lines from poetry, from prayers, the Bible. Life-lines, handed down. We live in a world of words. So, after a tragedy many survivors are lost! Pretty bleak. But it's good. Though not very kind in the circumstances, Mr Middlehoff. Or is it a warning you're giving me?'

'I would not presume.'

'Mmm . . . I know what you're saying and I'm doing my best.'

'Forgive me. The line is not specifically aimed at you Mr O'Hara. It is a line from a book I hope to write.'

'I heard you're a writer – but sure we're all writers here.'

'You, Mr O'Hara?'

'Yes. But like much of the rest of the country I don't put pen to paper. Too much talk here. But writers, we're all still writers.'

'Certainly story-tellers . . . raconteurs.'

'Story-tellers? Yes. Raconteurs? No. Makes us sound a bit false.'

'I'm sorry. I did not mean to offend you.'

'You didn't.'

'No harm done, then? As you say here.'

'Aha, and where did you pick that up?'

'I have become, of necessity, a jackdaw? Yes? Of expressions.'

'And what else have you picked up here?'

'More than you might imagine.'

'And tell me, Mr Middlehoff, are you happy here?'

'On and off.'

'Then you've learned more than you came with. Which I suppose is the purpose of exile.'

'So you will stay in this town?'

'Yes. And in the same house. I'll be carried out feet first, as we say.'

'Feet first?'

'In a coffin, Mr Middlehoff. Unlike the lad. I want to die at home when my time comes. Even though it's not been a lucky house for us. Let me ask you this, I'd like your opinion – you're a knowledgeable man. Do you think houses can break our spirit? Not through evil but through some old sorrow we know nothing about?'

'Perhaps. Strange things happen to houses. They are invaded. Sometimes their original purpose subverted.'

'Subverted?'

'Yes.'

'Well do you think they were always unlucky? Cursed in some way?'

'The long history of a house is indeed often thematic . . . Perhaps . . . I . . .'

'I see that even you're not certain. We loved that house. Maybe love isn't enough. We fought so hard to get it years ago. Well, we got it. When God wants to punish us He answers our prayers! Bitter thought. Unlucky houses. Unlucky families. Which comes first, do you think?'

I note the verbal commas and full stops that are often eccentrically placed in an Irish sentence.

38

Their conversation a tracery of question marks not always positioned to elicit information.

'I confess, Mr O'Hara, that I simply do not know.'

'That's honest. So, at the end of all this, Mr Middlehoff, will you sell me the gate?'

'I don't know that either, Mr O'Hara.'

'I'm aware the gate is valuable. But is it also special to you? Above the value? Is it more than a magnificent gate to you?'

'Perhaps.'

'How special?'

'I'm no longer sure.'

'So I've got a hope then?'

'Yes. Though I note you do not ask me where the gate has come from.'

'Its history, you mean? Because you're German?'

'Yes. Its history. Because I'm German.'

'Well, I'm going to take a gamble on that. And the lad had his own dreams, which he wove around that gate, so whatever history the gate had it's wreathed now in his dreams and it'll at least be one dream I bought him. And bad luck has had its way with us. Like I said, I need to give him something he loved. Do you understand?'

'I do.'

'Good. We have an understanding then?'

'Yes? Where would you put it? If I agree.'

'I'm going to put it at the entrance to the back garden, you know, where . . .'

'Yes. I know. I have spoken to Dr Carter . . .'

'Dr Carter did his best – his very best – but I know now what he probably knew then – there was no hope. No hope at all. He's a fine doctor, Carter. It's hard for him here, an English Protestant doctor. I've never felt that way myself but others do. They leave him to his own practice. It's good enough, I suppose, there's quite a number of Anglo-Irish around here. I admire the English in many ways. And we owe them a debt, a great debt. A harsh thing to say to you, Mr Middlehoff. Though it's not something we speak about much here, admiration of the English.'

'I've noticed. Dr Carter is an admirable man.'

'So is Dr Sullivan. Sullivan delivered the lad. Sullivan and matron. I remember the day well, my first son.'

'A man does not forget that day.'

'You have a son, Mr Middlehoff?'

I hesitate. On this subject I often do. It's a matter of tense.

'Yes.'

'I can see from your face I should go no further.'

'Thank you.'

'I must talk to Dr Carter properly and tell him of my appreciation. I suppose it makes it easier attending these things if you don't know the person, the body that was before. You both know more than I do about that. I bow my head. I couldn't do it. Couldn't look at it.'

'Of course not. You're his father.'

40

'Dr Sullivan would have found it very hard as well. Peacetime injuries is all he's had to train on I suppose, the odd tractor disaster. You and Dr Carter know other things. You've seen other sights. In that way you're linked.'

'In a way.'

'But from different sides.'

'Yes. But it's the same experience at the time.'

'And afterwards?'

'Different. Very different.'

'Victor and vanquished?'

'Yes. As you put it.'

'When they came to try to find – well you know – the lad lost his arm – when they came to try to find what was missing – to bury it with him – I sat on the wooden bench in the other yard way up from the back garden. Ah well, never thought I'd live to say such a line. Nothing was found. And poor Father Dwyer. I'm sure he was praying he'd find nothing. They're great on the search for truth when the answer is a prayer they know by heart. I sat on the bench on that unimaginable day, sky blue. A sky-blue day, eighty-eight degrees in a country unused to such temperatures, to such fierce light. The whole thing a dream. This can happen, I said to myself. This kind of death. And then I started thinking, what am I going to do with that back garden? Madness! The way the mind works in such circumstances. Foolish, unimportant details.'

'It is not madness. It is what protects the mind from madness.'

'You know that?'

'Yes.'

'We'll talk about it someday?'

'Perhaps.'

'I thought I'd brick it all up for a while. So I'd never put a foot in it again. Then I thought, no, just put up a wooden gate . . . then get someone to go in sometimes. Then I thought, who could I ask to do that place, that garden, for me? I mean, what lad could I pay a few shillings a week to and say, go in and weed it? They wouldn't want to. Then I set to wondering about Sissy's dream of a rose garden. All those years she'd been at me to do something about it. Make it into a proper garden. She was particularly keen on a rose garden. Wanted me to try to level it, you know. A garden? What do I know about gardens? But her aunt grew roses. Won prizes. Anyway, that's how my mind worked that day. That and other things, visions of the boy. I still don't know what to do with that back garden. I've put a kind of milky glass in the pantry window so that Sissy can't see the back garden even if she accidentally pulls the curtain. She didn't even comment. Not a word from her. She never goes into the back at all any more. Won't let anyone else go out either. Except me. The boys used to take it in turns to go out to the shed for the turf and coal – she was determined to burn no matter what the temperature. But she can't bear to see just Daragh going out. Alone.

42

But if I board the garden up, let it go to rack and ruin as they say, well, it'll become a wilderness. Rats will come.'

'Do not think like that Mr O'Hara.'

'Someone told me once flowers bloomed on graves. On even bits of . . . if you understand me.'

'I understand you.'

'And tell me, the shock of how shocking it is, does wear off? Yes?'

'I'm not sure.'

'Hasn't for you yet?'

'No. Did you know that we had a number of conversations? That your son would sometimes sit and talk to me as he awaited the island swimmers?'

'No, I didn't know that. He was proud to be asked to row the boat. It's been a club rule since the O'Driscoll child drowned. Oh, four years ago must be now. Her uncle, a Tralee man, up for the weekend was rowing the boat. Couldn't swim. Poor little Alice O'Driscoll fell off the boat – got into difficulties and went down. Some on the island and on the shore could hear the man, distraught, crying out his prayers, "Mary, Mary, Mother of God, save her. Save her." Shocking story. If the uncle could swim Alice would have lived. It wasn't the Mother of God who was needed that day. It was a swimmer! So that's what we decided to do with the lesson of Alice O'Driscoll and that's how Malachy Martin, the best swimmer in half the County of Kerry, got his promotion. Strings were pulled and we got a

Sergeant who in his spare time, and indeed in more than that, goes out to the lake to teach the town's children how to swim. Poor Malachy, he misses County Kerry. Told me it took him ages to get used to living in a place "without even a hint of the sea". Does something to the soul, he thinks. Have you ever heard him sing "Thank God We're Surrounded By Water"? He's got a great voice. Loves the sea and sent to a Midlands town. Isn't that the way? Ambition comes at a price. He divides swimmers into body types. Told Olivia she was for the breaststroke. Her shoulders, evidently. The lad's body was long, you know. His long arms made him a crawler. "Crawler's body, Tom. Long, narrow. The breaststroke boys are built differently, stockier, heavier, in my opinion, Tom." Who'd challenge him anyway? We learn from tragedy. Slowly. Anyway, I didn't know you'd chatted with the lad. He was shy in the beginning. Not like Olivia and as for Daragh, he's neither one nor the other. Hidden. But the lad – he was shy all right but good with . . .'

'Strangers?'

'Yes.'

'I thought he was a very kind boy.'

'He was. About the gate again: I want to mark the place with something important. Something he loved. And part of him is still there. Though they found nothing.'

★　★　★

'It's hard to know what to say to you Mr O'Hara.'

'I suppose it must be. To tell you the truth, I wouldn't know what to say myself. That's why poor Father Dwyer now says nothing. Perhaps it's best in these circumstances to say nothing. Or maybe there's a language we don't know yet. You speak two languages and yet you're stumped.'

'I speak four languages. This not to boast but to agree with you. "I'm stumped", as you put it, in all of them. And Mr O'Hara, I need to think about your request. If I decide to part with the gate I won't sell it. I will give it to you.'

'I did not come here for charity!'

'Forgive me. I did not mean . . .'

'I want to buy it. I want to buy it for him. A present for him. You wouldn't understand but I didn't buy a new bike for him. Bought him a second-hand bike. Last birthday. What meanness made me do that? He was grand about it but I knew he'd set his heart on the new one. Madness, the way my mind's working now. But I need to do this. I know it's an important thing, the gate. It's nearly eight feet high. The helmet is bronze. I'm not a fool. Though you may be surprised to hear it, my mother sculpted in bronze – exhibited in London, at the Royal Academy summer show, often. I know the gate's approximate value. And now I have the money.'

'I did not mean to suggest you did not.'

'Yes, you did. And normally you'd be right. I

have little money. I am the worst kind of poor man, a man who came from a family that was not rich – you know, we're not a rich country – but well off. Very well off indeed. Land. Which they sold. My mother's family, three sisters, two brothers all living and living well on the income from their capital. Freemen of the city of Dublin in recognition of their charitable work. My two uncles travelled the world. And I'm a world away from that now. And I'll never get back. A family can spin itself out, you know. I've seen it. I've lived it. Once upon a time and a twelve year time it was, as they say, there was me and my younger brother and my father and my mother – a small universe created in a mismatch. It split off and my mother went back to her grand house trailing two sons and we were trailed off, I suppose you could say, to boarding school and after a few years I ran away – to sea, as it happens – and when I got back she was dead. And there was no way back from that. I was lost in every way. They forgave, they said, but I made a few more mistakes. I seemed incapable of making the world bend to even my smallest wish. I shrugged my shoulders at the world, I suppose. I was a failure, Mr Middlehoff, at everything. At business, and they were generous to me helping me set up things – but nothing worked or maybe I just didn't care enough. Maybe one triumph is enough in life. And Sissy was mine. Anyway, back to money – the great subject for some people. Money has been made over to me as a balm I suppose. Not a lot. I'm still not reliable, you see. But I am not here as a pauper.'

'This isn't harsh patronage Mr O'Hara. If I part with the gate, and forgive me I need some time to think about it, it will be a gift to you. I liked the boy.'

'Who didn't?'

'You said at the inquest you knew he was playing with these things . . . these chemicals . . .'

'I did. It's no use now to talk of what I should have done.'

'I didn't mean to.'

'There was nothing in his head but crackpot ideas. Tell me a boy in the world who is without crackpot ideas? Olivia explained better than I did at the inquest. He was building a rocket. Bravado! It was a terrible accident. He was in heaven – strange phrase, I suppose, now – playing around with beakers and powders from school – and then Mr Kelly, the chemist, took a shine to him. Oh the lad was full of mad thoughts, childish thoughts of being a rocket scientist. For God's sake, when did an Irish Midlands town last produce a rocket scientist? Sure, have we ever produced any kind of scientist? Poets yes – and the lad loved poetry. They don't normally go together, they say, cleverness with words and at science, but they did with him. Anyway, the truth is, I didn't pay attention. Our little daughter was sick for a long time then we lost her less than a year ago. So. We weren't vigilant, Sissy and me. We missed the danger in what he was doing and we were punished for that. "His death is not a punishment, Tom," Bishop Fullerton told me. He didn't react well when I told him we were serving the toughest penance any priest could hand out and that it will never end. It's not his fault but somehow I felt Bishop Fullerton has let me down. Talked about the Risen Christ; strange choice of image for a father mourning his son. Anyway, the Risen Christ would heal the wound. Time, of course. He threw that old lie about time into the equation. To tell you the truth we were both a bit embarrassed at the end. But I know time will make no difference to us. He was ripped from us, you see – not like the long slow defeat with our little girl. It's like the difference between a deep sigh and a scream, I suppose. Not that I've screamed. Men don't much though I suppose you've heard them scream. In war. Wounds, I suppose.

'Yes.'

He looks away.

'Wounds! I dream myself, and I'm not a woman, of remaking his body. I dream of putting it together again. And I only imagine how he was after it happened. In the morgue – well, they dressed him up. What's there to say? I feel as if we've sent him back to God, unmade, as if we were careless and sent him back to Him broken; as if someone had given us a precious vase to look after, rare, like one of those vases my uncles would bring back from the East, irreplaceable, and one day you just move its position, carelessly, casually, not paying due attention to what it is was you have in your hand, and it falls and smashes! That's how I feel. Careless. We were careless. We didn't look after it, I mean him, properly. We weren't vigilant. Sorry. I'm struggling . . .'

'It's understandable, Mr O'Hara.'

'Do you . . . do you just struggle along yourself with life Mr Middlehoff?'

'We all do.'

'The bishop would tell you of the Risen Christ. The Great Survivor. No good to you, I suppose?'

'I'm not familiar with that particular . . . incarnation.'

'Well, ask Bishop Fullerton. He'll give you a lecture on it. You play chess with him every month they say. We don't have much call for chess here. Bishop Fullerton went to Trinity, you know – Protestant university – unusual for a Catholic boy – had to get special permission – but not unheard of. And his was a late, well late-ish, vocation. He moved around with the English. His sister married an English peer though he rarely refers to it. Naturally. Anyway, I must go now. Thank you for talking to me. It's the act of a gentleman. Will you think about the gate?'

'I will.'

'And will you think about a price?'

'No. As I said, it can only be a gift Mr O'Hara. Otherwise I will not part with it. But if I decide to give it to you then you must organise the removal.'

'Saving my pride are you?'

'I admire you Mr O'Hara, and though I am very sad at what has happened I am not acting out of pity.'

'Pity? What's wrong with pity? "A pity beyond all telling is hid in the heart of love." Do you know that line?'

'No.'

'Yeats. And he's right: at the heart of deep love you'll find a kind of pity. I can see you don't agree.'

'No. But I will consider the idea.'

'There's a lot to consider in that little idea. And thank you about the gate. Considering it, at least. Like I said, you've been a gentleman to me. I won't forget.'

'You're Irish, Mr O'Hara. Forgetfulness is not possible.'

'And you're German, Mr Middlehoff. No doubt memory is a burden.'

A sudden word-wound? No. A simple statement of fact. We say goodbye. I wait in the courtyard as he walks to his car and watch as with some difficulty he manoeuvres himself back into the driver's seat as though he were again assuming a crouched position in a cage. His hands grip the wheel with an intensity that suggests he is more likely to pull it free from the dashboard than guide it through the various movements necessary

50

to its journey through the main gates which, with a kind of perverse confidence, I keep open during the day. And once through those gates he must turn left towards the home where his past is waiting for him.

CHAPTER 3

She is here. Harriet Calder is here. Mostly she is not. It is thus that I define my life, in major and in minor matters. I am. She is not. I drive carefully, for example. She does not. She drives, as she does most things, recklessly. She trusts her luck perhaps. In this we are very different. When she is not with me she is yet with me. She is my shadow-self, which I can neither catch nor detach myself from. She is the darker side of me.

Harriet Calder is here! I breathe the same air as she. She is not my type. She is thin and what in youth seemed a pleasing coltishness now, in early middle age, seems like a disconcerting lack of femininity. Her height does not help. I am a tall man and though she is not as tall as I her habit of wearing her hair loosely pulled and piled and pinned on top of her head makes her appear closer to my height than is the fact.

She is wearing a red jacket. It is, as I know, an old hunting jacket. Her legs are encased in narrow black slacks and, swinging from her shoulders, a rain cape, which resembles one of

Bridget's rain capes. What on Bridget looks merely useful, on Harriet looks daring. Harriet is a challenge and despite her slightly androgynous appearance many men wish to respond. My sexual jealousy is deep and permanent. It is an emotion to which Harriet has never given any consideration. Her terms prevail. I am, and have always acknowledged myself to be, helpless. That is the difference between my brother and I. Heinrich, in thrall to his wife Carlotta, rebels against his sentence. I do not. I know that Harriet's need of me is less than my need of her. The degree is irrelevant. I was not always so wise. Few are. They believe the terms can be renegotiated. They are wrong.

She's pounded, cape flying, down the wood-panelled hallway like an army of one. I follow slowly. She is here. That is all. That is everything. She throws the cape, though it is wet, over the high back of a dark green library arm chair. She sees the book of poetry lying on the side table. Gottfried Benn. *Morgue.* She puts it carefully back on the small Biedermeier table and the lamplight shines on it. I keep this room lighted, though dimly, day and night, summer and winter.

'What was it your father said about your obsessive poetry reading, Thomas?'

'Hardly excessive, Harriet. Besides, he encouraged me in this.'

'As in many things.'

'Yes. Drink, Harriet?'

'At eleven-thirty in the morning? Certainly, Thomas.'

'Whiskey?'

'Perfect.'

She smiles at me. When Harriet smiles she inclines her head, her lips twist slightly at the corners and then her rather crooked front teeth are exposed in the smile. Her smile. What can I say? Harriet's smile. Even in this attempt to describe the smile of Harriet Calder I am aware that I am a man obsessed. Now the red jacket is thrown over the arm of another chair. The grey jersey she is wearing reveals nothing of the figure beneath. She is a hidden woman. In this she has ruined other women for me. Gender ostentation is, as I have found, often the result of gender uncertainty. Nothing can be secret when all is on display, and it is within secrecy that obsession lies. Harriet's body. The disproportion of legs to torso: I know it well. I pour the whiskey and turn towards this woman for whom my sexual desire has never ceased. Since the first time I made love to Harriet Calder, which was the first time I made love. She wore white. We were shocked. She was in mourning for her parents who'd been killed in a car crash. My family – her distant relatives – had expected black. I turn away from the memory. She is speaking. I love her. I hate her. I listen to her.

'Now remind me, indulge me, Thomas. What was your father's line?'

'He said I suck poets dry.'

'Very clever man, your father.'

'Yes.'

'He must miss Ursula. He won't remarry?'

'Harriet, he's an old man. He has lost two wives. My mother and Ursula. Besides, he honours their memory.'

'So much easier isn't it, honouring the memory than honouring your wife when she's alive?'

'Or husband!'

'Ah! Yes. I do my best, Thomas. There are lives between us. And I come to you often.'

'Not often enough, and you refuse to live with me.'

'Yet I'm here. From time to time I too must be with you. I'd like another whiskey.'

Then she settles herself on a low sofa.

'You know I despise this place, Thomas. This house. I hate its deliberate isolation. Its grey stone. Its windows looking out onto that grey lake. I hate everything that's false about it. The obviousness of your choice. It's lost, that time, Thomas. Proust is a bore and a thief, like you. With your pathetic scraps of memory – semblance of things past. The squirrel is of the rat family, Thomas. I hate it and its habits. I hate this place.'

I remain calm. I know this game. It's solo. She is here. That is my triumph. It is enough. It is not enough. It is, however, all I will have. I can suffer her rage. It rarely lasts for long; it will abate and return. Suddenly she sighs.

'I'm sorry about the boy. You sounded upset.'

'I was. I am.'

'Was there an inquest?'

'Yes.'

'And?'

'Nothing really. A shocking accident.'

'What age was he?'

'Sixteen, almost seventeen.'

'Christ!'

She downs her whiskey. I never try to stop her. She knows her limits. I have never seen her drunk.

'Good God, I recognise that portrait! That's from the hunting lodge. You didn't have that the last time I was here.'

'Which is too long ago.'

'For God's sake, Thomas! I owe you nothing. Nothing! And yet still I come to you. I travel by boat, which I hate just slightly less than I hate flying. Always a foul crossing, a brutal sea. I drive through these ugly towns and villages. It's bungalow hell. What terror do these people have of being too far from the ground? Some peasant lust for the earth? Bungalows everywhere. And grey after grey: it makes the place seem like a mirage. This rubbish about green! For heaven's sake, how could you spot green through the driving grey rain?'

And she rages, again. I stand motionless. I remain silent. She is here.

'I do all this to come here. That is essential. If you came to me, Thomas, we know what would happen. You are a man who might not leave. You are a man who could not leave once. This is a good agreement. It is a good arrangement. Islands, close but separate. And that ghastly Irish Sea. It must always be difficult to get to you. We've done well with this elective distance between us. In this, at least, we did well. Would you say I come to make love to you, Thomas? To make love? To you? What a phrase! "Make love." Who the hell can make love? People make bread, jam, babies. Who the hell makes love? Not us, Thomas. Not us.'

I know I must stay silent. Is that not a sign of love? To stand silent against the onslaught? To endure? To let her rage flow? To allow it to flow so that it does not engulf her? To know the point at which to pull her back? A man in love does this. I am consumed by her. Do I truly love her? The way I truly loved my wife? I wish I'd never met her. I wish I'd never met Harriet Calder. When she is here with me I wish I'd never met her. When she is not here with me I wish I'd never met her. I wish for a life without her in it. But I live such a life. Perhaps I love her too much? Is that possible? Well, is it? She is burning a little now with the whiskey. I know this woman. Is that all that it is? To know the woman? She looks at me, that sudden look, and then it's gone. Soon we will go upstairs. She will run up and I will walk slowly. She will turn around quickly. Then she will strip, the way a boy strips. I will lock the door, as I always do. I will lean back against the door as I always do, for support, and she will throw herself on me and we will be lost. Again.

My bed is large and old. We do not share a bed. It is a place we go to. It is a territory we invade and then abandon, like absentee landlords. Its iconic position in marriage, the bed in the couple's room, the theatre where all is played out, is the symbol not of sexuality but of coupling. 'The bed I built can never be moved for it is built around the trunk of a deep-rooted olive tree.' Odysseus returning to Penelope. The great complicated secret of the bed known only to them. And it was thus she knew he was indeed her husband. There is always a secret between couples, sometimes within it lies the seed of their destruction. I stand behind her and unpin her hair. She bows her head.

'Harriet,' I whisper.

'Say nothing, Thomas. Say nothing.'

CHAPTER 4

The letter lies on my study table. My father's handwriting has always seemed to me to be in exquisite contrast to his character. It is spidery-light, as though the writer cared more about the hieroglyphics than the content; a deception, for few men weigh their words or their actions more carefully than my father.

September 18th, 1962

Dear Thomas,

I have taken a long time to reply to you. It is always an exercise in exactitude to write to you in English, which would now seem to be your chosen tongue.

And I send this letter to Ireland, your elective country of exile, to which, driven by grief and anger, you have retreated. I use the word 'retreat' with the care for language that befits the son of a respected lexicographer. I also note, with some satisfaction, a certain genetic imperative in your own missive, indeed in all your work. I accede, Thomas, to your wish to have

59

access to my notes on the subject of Ireland. I have, after all, abandoned the subject.

The title of my book on Ireland was to have been 'The Weapons of the Country'. I have collated my notes under three headings: Language; Love; Memory. They have been forwarded to you separately by parcel post. We are an efficient nation. It is our secondary characteristic, perhaps. Secondary characteristics when applied with concentrated power to a cause, whatever the nature of that cause, have played a greater part in history than is ever allowed. The secondary characteristic of the Irish? I leave that to you, Thomas. The Irish mind was formed in the ancient language of the Celt. Its roots, as you are aware, are Sino-Indian. Perhaps, therefore, the Irish mind is partly an occidental mind? Mr Yeats has something to say on the subject. The English language, however, a gift foolishly handed to them by the British, but on the point of a sword, has been wielded by the Irish with exquisite ferocity against their old enemy. Remember, it is their first weapon.

I now accept that, as you intimated in your letter, I have always been rather wary of writing this book. Perhaps I felt a certain sensitivity in acknowledging that I first visited Dublin in 1939–40 for the purpose of a (comparatively modest) undertaking in espionage. Which failed. It is true we were outmanoeuvred, thwarted by those who, in understanding the nature and the language of treachery even better than we did, quietly and effectively subverted our plan to subvert the IRA to our own cause. Hitler's decision, driven by geography, made strategic sense. The outcome, however, is often determined by a nation's historical memory. In the case of Ireland the symphonic note of their national dirge creates a tinnitus of the soul. They were deaf to all else.

Finally, in relation to this book may I challenge you as to the purity of your own timing? What has happened to your planned second book on Gottfried Benn? Why desert Benn? You have much to say on the subject of the divided self, and Benn's autobiography *Doppelleben* is of historical as well as literary importance. So why do you dedicate yourself to a book on Ireland? It is less than five years since Heinrich Böll published *Irisches Tagebuch*, his partly enchanted impression of his many visits to Galway's Achill Island, a work I regard as more provocative than its rather anaemic title would suggest. However, it is the teller not the tale. Why now? Could it be that you desire to become further lost in the history of another country? You should remember that Paul Celan, whom you admire and who remains my obsession kept faith with language and the German language 'through the thousand darknesses of murderous speech'. That he should honour this belief in its power though both parents perished in the labour camps compels me to examine unceasingly the shattered silence of his work.

To family matters – briefly. You enquire as to my health. You were always courteous. My death is not imminent. It is, however, a discernible shape on the horizon. We need not be more dramatic. To Heinrich. He has again separated from Carlotta. Perhaps you are already aware of this? It is possible he sees himself as an Houdini of the heart, endlessly tying and untying himself. He returns, I believe, because in the taming of Carlotta's wildness he is as close to virtue as he will ever come. Vice may bind but its shackles rust. 'Does one bring up sons to have them ruined by a woman?' – your mother's cry after the announcement of this too-young engagement. It is very difficult to see one's son choose a woman like Carlotta. Your own choice of Veronika brought for a time the deepest joy to us both. I will not go further. I am not a sadist. While Heinrich is a constant source of worry, I am at ease with him. With you, Thomas, I have always experienced a certain tension. It existed even before the estrangement that followed Frederick's death and Veronika's collapse, and later, of course, her death. Poor Frederick. Poor Veronika.

You should marry again. You should have another child. Perhaps you will regard this advice with contempt. Perhaps you will interpret it as an encouragement to predatory love. You have deeper knowledge of this subject than many men. Ethics and love? Are there ethics in love, Thomas? Again, a question to which you are perhaps best equipped to give an answer, having destroyed your family for Mrs Calder, as she calls herself now. Legitimately, I know. Though not in my eyes. I remain bitter. Forgive me. I have again into your current unmarried state obtruded. The siege is over I assume? You have admitted defeat? Mrs Calder is reluctant to take possession of her territory? Perhaps I am wrong in this. No? Again, forgive me. The cry of the father through time.

Your father,
Erik

On re-reading this letter I note its lack of warmth. Not a surprise to either of us. As a gesture I gift you my first edition of A. M. Sullivan's 1868 *Speeches from the Dock*. It will be sent separately to you. Only in Ireland could a book with such a title become a bestseller. It may help you understand the essence of their 'holy hatred' – John Mitchel's phrase. He was exiled in shackles. Holy hatred: start from there. Erik

CHAPTER 5

My monthly chess game with Bishop Fullerton presents not only an intellectual but a philosophical challenge to him. Since over 90 per cent of the population is Roman Catholic, and thus his spiritual authority is rarely challenged, he relishes the occasional doubter. His little 'Doubting Thomas' joke, however, has been dropped, to our mutual relief.

I check the fire and then the supper arrangements. Linen napkins, to the laundering of which Bridget pays such attention, cover in their starched perfection two plates of sandwiches and one large silver platter on which rests a ginger cake that Bridget has baked for the bishop especially. This minor feast has been carefully set out on a side table, 'in case the bishop gets hungry after the game'. Which he always does. He is, I think, a permanently hungry man and souls alone do not satisfy him. We start at nine-thirty. He has dined earlier, as have I, yet the sandwiches and cake remain essential. Bridget has today made her own brown bread and soda bread. Some time ago she had been informed by the bishop's housekeeper that he regards country butter with particular favour. I loathe it. The guest's desires, however, are paramount. So after my monthly chess game with the bishop I will eat, for politeness' sake, at least one cold-meat sandwich made with Bridget's soda bread – the thin-slicing of which she has informed me is difficult – and I will watch the bishop devour the rest.

I see the lights of a car. Our evening is about to begin. Bishop Fullerton will have been driven from the Bishop's Palace, as it is known, to Lake House at no doubt excessive speed by Eamonn McNamara. Eamonn, who has acquired a reputation for 'foot-on-the-accelerator madness', pulls up with a flourish, his arrival signalled by the screech of brakes. He leaps from the car and with a slight incline of his head, not exactly a bow, he opens his passenger's door and guides the bishop out of his jet-black, newest-model Mercedes.

'Good evening Thomas! How I look forward to tonight's challenge. I must warn you, Thomas, I'm geared up. Isn't that right, Eamonn? I'm geared up for victory.'

'You are, Bishop, you are indeed. Oh yes, Mr Middlehoff, tonight's the night.'

'Good evening, Eamonn.'

'Now Eamonn, you go home to Margaret and the children and shall we say eleven-ish? Is that all right, Eamonn?'

'Of course, Bishop.'

As Eamonn executes one of his top-speed

mechanical pirouettes and races down the drive Bishop Fullerton smiles indulgently and progresses down the hallway, the skirts of his robes almost touching the wainscoting. In the study he settles into his usual chair.

'Ah this room! How I admire this room. I admire this house. I always did. You did well to buy it. Poor Edmond Pennington. I know he's taken up his estates in England – all very grand, I'm told – but I feel certain that even after all these years he longs for Lake House. Still, primogeniture, that somewhat brutal system of inheritance the British practise, might make one a little ambivalent about the untimely death of a childless elder brother. Or is that uncharitable of me? Ah, what a great fire Bridget makes. The Irish love a fire. Have you noticed, Thomas?'

'Indeed.'

'I hear Tom O'Hara came to see you.'

I sigh. What more can I do? The information system in an Irish town would put the British Secret Service to shame, and frequently did.

'Yes.'

'Surprising. Coming to see you. I mean, he hardly knows you. We're all trying to help him. He's busy saving Sissy, I suppose.'

The bishop, who is possessive by nature, does not, I think, like to contemplate the dilution of his exclusive relationship, as he sees it, with 'The German' by even the possibility of a friendship that I might develop with one of his parishioners.

Particularly one who is grieving and should rightly find all the comfort he needs in his belief in God and in the support of God's emissaries of whom, in this town, the bishop is the most exalted.

'And his children.'

'Yes. But Sissy, she's the one.'

There is always a certain relief in the discussion of another's tragedy. Sympathy flows like a balm between those who speak of tales of agony to which they have been but distant witnesses.

'Are you saying a man can only save one person at a time, Bishop? Even a father?'

'I'm not wise enough for these things. I try, of course. Marriage is a mysterious country to me. I always felt the climate would be too intense and the language rather difficult to learn. My guidance is in theological matters, sometimes in matters of philosophy but not in matters psychological.'

'Whiskey?'

'Thank you! *Uisce beatha*! The water of life. To you, Thomas, and to chess and to conversation. I often think, Thomas, that it's the conversation that I most appreciate about these monthly jousts.'

He beams at me.

'I'm not the Pope, but sometimes my flock listens to me as though every word is spoken *ex cathedra*. It's a heavy responsibility. This is only a chair from which I pronounce when I'm here with you.'

He is pleased with his little joke and continues, 'My flock rarely challenges me.'

'The sheep rarely challenge the shepherd.'

'Sheep, is it? How little you know us Thomas. They do not challenge me in religious debate, but they can slip under the net.'

'Or pen.'

'Oh very good, Thomas, very good. Yes, they can slip away from me. This green velvet winged beauty,' and he pats the chair, 'I wish I could have one like this in the Palace. But as I told you, my predecessor Bishop Heggarty was rather austere. Got rid of quite a lot. So it's difficult for me to go out now and acquire such a piece. It would look too opulent. Send out the wrong message. We're an army. And in public, indeed even in private, we're mostly on parade. Forgive the military analogy. When I was training for the priesthood the lecture that made the most impression on me emphasised that "sinners have in a sense lost their way, like soldiers marching in the army of God – who perhaps went AWOL and then couldn't find their way back". It was given by the then Bishop of Galway, as I recall. He was speaking to the assembled first-year students. "Sin," he said, "is indeed like getting lost in a maze and each way you turn you can't get out. That's the habitual sinner for you: lost in a maze." And some bright spark had piped up "no sense of direction" and we all laughed. He did too. Loud, booming laugh as befits a bishop, eh Thomas?'

'Indeed.'

'When we'd calmed down a bit the Bishop looked at us all. Right round the room you

69

know – catching each lad's eye, so to speak. "Exactly, gentlemen, exactly," he said. "Gentlemen", that got us, the word "gentlemen". "Bear in mind, my young sports, that you've got to have journeyed somewhere before you've a sense of direction to lose. You've come, most of you, from country towns and villages or farms on the edge of nowhere. You're barely out of your teens and we're going to turn you into commanding officers of the souls of others. That's our task here in Maynooth, to turn a bunch of youngsters into soldiers of the Lord and I've as much trouble, I can tell you, as any Sergeant Major." We laughed, but we didn't forget it. We knew we'd have power, great power over men. The greatest. The power of forgiveness or not: "Whose sins thou shalt forgive, they are forgiven them; and whose sins thou shalt retain, they are retained." Power! That's what he was telling us we had. And that people would obey.'

'Is it not possible that much of the obedience is driven by fear?'

I carefully position the chess board between us and set up.

'Fear and love perhaps, Thomas. Not a bad combination, as Machiavelli would agree. You look surprised. We are not completely unaware of Machiavelli here.'

'And I would say that God is more feared than loved here.'

'Do you not fear where you love, Thomas?'

I pause. I do indeed fear where I love.

'I see where you have led me.'

'Checkmate! As you usually say to me.'

'Congratulations. Do you believe every sinner can be saved and every non-believer is a potential convert?'

'That's the business.'

He parries well. We have got our rhythm now and I enjoy the sparring.

'Profitable?'

'Very. Spiritually, Thomas, spiritually. The Irish Catholic Church is not now, nor has it ever been, corrupt. May I just say how I admire your taste in whiskey. You've gone native, as they say. Very good. Though I see you keep the other as well. You're a careful man. I have had a difficult, very difficult, day. I decided to talk to the Brothers Enda and Rory – to others, but mostly to them – at the college. They taught the O'Hara lad. Science and History and English. They teach with passion. Too much, according to some, particularly May Garvey and Bogus Brogan – they're neighbours of the O'Haras. Do you know them?'

'I have met Mr Brogan once – at the funeral.'

'Ah – well, they're a bit competitive with each other. May writes a bit. She resented the small success Dennis Brogan had a year or so ago and she started to call him Bogus Brogan, and it stuck. Bogus takes it in good heart. But they're both on the same side when it comes to the teaching of history. She had to give up teaching when she got

71

married, but does a bit, helping before exams, and Bogus teaches out at St Patrick's. Anyway, after my conversation today I think with a few of the Brothers she may have a point. Still, I'm aware that a shadow of shame can fall on men in a country that has been long over-run – a feeling that somehow they should have prevented the humiliation. Such a nation needs its heroes as it builds itself from scratch. Which Ireland has done. You'll give us that, Thomas – yes?'

'It is a great achievement.'

'Yes, we've done very well. Church and State have created a philosophically and spiritually united country. Much of that has been achieved in less than forty years. Much of it due to an outstanding education system based on the Christian Brothers and the nuns. We rely on their vocations. They're clever men: redoubtable Brother Gogarty, for example – brilliant man. I was talking to him today – double first in mathematics from UCD. He should have been a Jesuit, of course: would have suited his mind better. God works in mysterious ways. I managed a quick chat with Brother Anselm Corrigan who teaches English to the younger boys – reluctantly nominates William Shakespeare greatest play-wright while implying that his mother might have been Irish! Joke, Thomas, joke.'

And he roars again like a satisfied lion. He is after all king of the spiritual jungle here. His laughter has the explosive quality he believes suitable to a bishop and to which I have had to make adjustment since my first alarming experience of its reverberation. He will now wish to develop his theme. The game will commence late this evening. I will, however, still find it difficult to resist the temptation to dispatch him with speed. Good manners demand that I do not make too obvious my superiority at the game.

'But it's Brothers Enda and Rory I really wanted to talk to. That pair – they were twinned at birth – when God made them he matched them. Do you know that expression, Thomas?'

'No, it is new to me.'

'Take it as a gift, Thomas . . .' With a sigh he continues, 'Well it's the first week back. The pupils have had a terrible shock; we've all had a terrible shock, of course. There are rumours – oh, not many – and some disquiet, I suppose you could call it. About such matters we are normally silent here, having learned perhaps that it is wiser. Still, you know, an explosion – such a thing has a kind of after-effect. That resurgence of trouble in the North a few years ago – that was a surprise, I suppose you could say – well it's now virtually petered out. There'd been decades of peace in a reasonably contented Republic, civil war behind us and the North – no pleasure you know, but settled into a waiting game – as we saw it anyway. I always say that history will give us the North. A confusing phrase but you know what I mean. The British always leave in the end. Time is on our side.'

I try to resist all conversations about history, whether ancient, medieval or modern. I will write

73

my book and remain silent. Whereof we cannot speak, we sometimes write.

'. . . though from what I've heard Brothers Enda and Rory believe time needs a bit of help, a kind of hurry-up message. They're from Ballinasloe. It's a great little town, Ballinasloe. I've got distant cousins there, the McGreevey twins. Grand lads – discovered their vocation for the priesthood in the same year Brothers Enda and Rory went off to training college to become Christian Brothers. It was bumper year, that year in Ballinasloe. Brother Enda's vocation is, he believes, a more passionate calling than most – that his vocation empowers him to create the future soul of his country. Though he's no Joyce. Thank God. He is a fanatical teacher. A powerful man in a community, particularly here. "You only get one chance with a boy to send them out blazing with love of their country," he declared, and admonished me to remember, a little impertinently I felt but I let it go, what Pearse said, that "the Irish mind is the clearest mind that has ever applied itself to the consideration of nationality and of national freedom . . . It was characteristic of Irish-speaking men that when they thought of the Irish nation they thought less of its outer forms and pomps than of the inner thing which was its soul." Brother Enda's right, of course, it's all about the soul, though his tone was a little arrogant. And a bishop must encourage humility.'

Here he smiled. The smile of a fat man is often

less open to misinterpretation than that of a man whose skin is drawn tight over angular features, as mine is, yet there remains something sly in his expression.

'So I thought I'd bring him down a peg or two. I mentioned . . . oh, I don't remember how,' he smiles again, 'but I managed to bring in Brother Gogarty's first in mathematics: not normally our forte. He didn't like that.' And the bishop relished the memory of his small triumph and continued, 'Well that started Brother Enda! The Pearse quotations tumbled from his lips: '"An heroic tale is more essentially a factor in education than a proposition from Euclid!' Tell that to Brother Gogarty, Bishop." "But sure you see him all the time Brother Enda, you tell him." "I will," he said, "and I'll remind him of Pearse on the subject of Lady Aberdeen's mathematical abilities." Do you know that quote, Thomas?'

'Alas no.'

'"It is further known," wrote Pearse, and I like this one myself, "that a pound a week is sufficient to sustain a Dublin family in honest hunger – at least very rich men tell us so, and very rich men know all about everything, from art galleries to the domestic economy of the tenement room. I would ask those who know that a man can live and thrive, can house, feed, clothe and educate a large family on a pound a week to try the experiment themselves. Let them show how the thing is done . . . they will drink their black tea with

75

gusto and masticate their dry bread scientifically (Lady Aberdeen will tell them the proper number of bites per slice); they will write books on 'How to be Happy though Hungry'; when their children call out for more food they will smile." Brilliant, that bit of satire by Pearse. He's a hero, no doubt about it. But to Brother Enda he's more than that. It seemed essential to remind the good Brother of the sin of idolatry but nothing stopped him. Said he wasn't worthy to kiss Pearse's feet. I assured him no one was going to ask him to go that far. Is this boring you Thomas?'

'No. Not at all, Bishop. Does he teach any history other than Irish history?'

'Oh indeed. The Reformation – not a period to be celebrated in a Catholic country.'

'No doubt he has his own version.'

'Ah we must not mock Brother Enda.' And the bishop smiles that sly smile again. 'He tells the boys English lust destroyed the Catholic faith in England.'

'Lust is not a specifically British characteristic.'

'Oh I agree Thomas, but English lust! It is Brother Enda's opinion that you'd not find an Irishman destroying the Catholic faith for a woman.'

'Is it not true, Bishop, that the greatest woman in Ireland is Cathleen Ní Houlihan? Does she not become young and beautiful when she has lured the young groom away to fight for her – for Ireland – in Mr Yeats's play?'

'Ah, wouldn't you charm the birds Thomas! We appreciate it when a newcomer – because you're no longer a stranger here, you've moved up in the pantheon – pronounces our most beloved names correctly. I'll give you another: Roisín Dubh – dark Irish rose – how about that for the name of a country?'

'Enchanting.'

'The poet, seventeenth century I believe, was originally talking about his love – I suppose we stole his pet name for her and gave it to Ireland. Isn't it a lovely thing to name your country after a woman? We gave her all those women's names so that when we sang our rebel songs, even at a time when we sang them in Gaelic, the English wouldn't know what we were singing about. We know what love is. It's deep and enduring and requires sacrifice. It's not lust, which is just a surrender to our baser nature. That's one of my most popular sermons. I'm talking too much. Forgive me, I suppose I'm talking the encounter out of me in order to understand it better . . . Shall we start?'

After a short, not wholly companionable, silence we commence our game. His defeat is swift.

'No! How did you do that? You win again! I sometimes feel I come here for the good of my soul. Yes, ritual humiliation is good for the soul. It teaches one humility, which I must then teach others.'

'A bishop needs humility?'

77

'Most particularly a bishop.'

'Another whiskey?' I know he will say yes. He finishes the whiskey quickly.

'I am armed now and I'm ready again for battle, Thomas.'

'What an alarming prospect, Bishop.'

The explosive laughter again. I smile and demolish him. An uncharacteristic revelation of my contempt for the inadequacy of his game. He is hurt. I have been foolish. We sit in silence for a moment. Distraction is required. He picks up a book from a small side table.

'And is that Mr Böll's work I see here? *Irisches Tagebuch* – "Irish Journal". Thomas? Following in eminent footsteps. And what's this I see? *Speeches from the Dock*, A. M. Sullivan and, I do believe, a first edition. That's a treasure you've got; all the great speeches there: Theobald Wolfe Tone, Robert Emmet, the Sheares brothers, hanged together while holding hands, Charles Joseph Kickham . . . The list is endless.'

He settles back in the armchair in which my father once sat. On which Harriet carelessly threw her wet cape, on which once I lay while she held me in her mouth for . . . How long was it? Sexual timelessness. Inaccurate memories of the dream. I get up abruptly.

'Forgive me, Bishop. I need to check something.'

'Of course, Thomas.' Then he settles down to my books.

I close the door gently and lean against the table

in the hall. I hold its edges too tightly. I must control this sudden desperation to see Harriet Calder. I have much practice. When I come back he looks pensively at me. Is there something in my face? Bishop Fullerton is a man who searches daily for traces of a man's soul in his face. He is a spiritual cartographer of the physiognomy. I may be the master at chess, a fact he resents, but I feel that he could position a man on his moral ladder with far greater expertise than he places his queen or pawn.

'A little supper, Bishop?'

We move to the sideboard where, with a flourish, he unveils the sandwiches and the cake.

'Did you mind me doing that? Ahhh! isn't Bridget a saint . . . lower case, Thomas. A woman's touch! Did I ever tell you that I once considered marriage?'

He is determined on this intimacy. His conversational ship has left port. It will take time to anchor him again. I can wait. As we take our plates back and I attend to the fire he begins his story.

'I was about twenty-four, in the year of my vocation. A late vocation, in a sense. I met her at university – we were friends. Aisling was her name and she *was* a vision. Clever too. But despite her infinitely careful encouragement over many months . . . well, shall we say I resisted. She married my cousin a few years later. They are not happy, my mother tells me, but they soldier on; they soldier on. We believe in endurance in these matters. You come from another world. Another set of rules apply here between men and women. Temptation, of course, comes to us all, but is easier to resist when the conscience is trained by a loving God. I do appreciate the discretion with which, I'm told, you entertain your female companions. You avoid scandal.'

I am appalled at this astonishing invasion of my privacy. I experience a momentary desire to respond. It passes. I must not forget that I now live in a sexually repressed, deeply religious, very small town. I must and do respect its proprieties. I have every intention of continuing to be discreet. After a tense moment or two during which he gleans that I do not intend to comment he continues.

'Ah well, tomorrow I visit Sissy O'Hara. It won't be easy.'

'No,' I say and sit down opposite him again.

'You were at the funeral – you knew the boy?'

'I met him. Not often. In fact the last time I saw him he talked of Pearse and indeed Sarsfield.'

'Patrick Sarsfield! Earl of Lucan – one of my favourite heroes. When his own name was whispered to him as the password didn't he throw it down like a gauntlet in front of his enemies when he relieved the siege of Limerick? That man had everything: wealth, brilliance and they say he was very good looking. He died later on the battlefield in France, crying out, "Oh that this was for

Ireland." So he talked of Sarsfield as well as Pearse?'

'Yes – I found it moving. If a little unsettling.'

'And why would it unsettle you?'

'Such passion. Such competition with his sister to know by heart speeches, rhetoric.'

'Well I've told Brother Enda to calm the rhetoric a bit. I'm considering talking to the powers that be about a transfer for that pair, maybe to Dundalk or Drogheda. Might suit their temperaments better. Very passionate towns up there; they'll feel more at home. I know it was a terrible accident and that any teenage boy, as they call them now, could lay his hands on a chemistry set – maybe more – still, after what happened in the North . . . in that pathetic campaign. Yes, minds were twisted there, just after we'd all settled down, though never giving up our legitimate hopes for the future. But there's a world of difference between a free nation building its soul on the tales of men who fought hard and long against a ruthless oppressor and breaking young minds with the weight of old sadnesses and burdening young shoulders with an unpayable debt to ghosts. Do you know how Pearse said you appease a ghost, Thomas?'

'No Bishop, I do not.'

'You give it what it asks.'

'A dangerous concept.'

'Indeed it is, Thomas. It's *Hamlet*, of course.'

'Who was unequal to the task: "an oak tree planted in a costly vase".'

81

'Goethe! It's marvellous to talk to you Thomas. This conversation with you will help me tomorrow when I visit the O'Haras, to begin to help them to forget.'

'I doubt they will ever do that.'

'If they allow themselves to be lost in God's love they will remember differently. An embarrassing concept to you, no doubt.'

I cannot resist feeling angry in some obscure way.

'My father said there were four things a man or a nation could do with their history, which is, after all, their collective memory.'

'Well now, you have me fascinated, Thomas.'

I proffer the whiskey.

'No! I couldn't. Oh, all right then. Eamonn will be cross with me. Just a splash. Continue. Not with the whiskey. With the story.'

His small brown eyes behind the glasses he dons for chess can sometimes glitter with a concentrated hunger.

'My father said a nation could forget, exploit, obscure or live with its history.'

'What a succinct appraisal. Wouldn't I have loved to meet your father.'

I note that he uses the past tense.

'He rarely leaves Germany now.'

He has realised his mistake. Coughs, puts his glass carefully on the table. There is an uneasy silence between us now. The Bishop does not know how to deal with the history of my country. But then who does? He sighs and I watch to see him search for another subject, perhaps related in some way to what we currently discuss so that there will be no implication of a too-abrupt cessation.

'My sister's husband fought in the First and Second World War. Is it indelicate to mention this?'

'Not at all, Bishop.' I am surprised he does not use the common terminology 'The Emergency' to describe the Second World War.

'He's a peer, you know. Much older than Deirdre. But I must say they seem happy. She met him in Dublin. His cousin was shot dead in front of his wife that terrible Sunday morning, 21 November 1920. Though he didn't tell my sister for years. Thought it might kill the romance, I suppose. Michael Collins ordered the squad – the "Twelve Apostles"; never liked that name, obviously – to kill army spies from Dublin Castle. Hard to look a man straight in the face – which I suppose you must – and pull the trigger with his wife standing there screaming. Managed eighteen, they say, or was it fourteen? – it's debated. They say he hoped the British would retaliate. He got his wish. They opened fire later the same day in Croke Park at a Gaelic football match. Thirteen killed, including three children. Bloody Sunday, they called it. The Anglo-Irish War: long, long and bloody story. Ah it must be the whiskey. I'm lost in history again. I didn't expect to tell you that, about my sister and her husband, I mean. Nor about his cousin. It shall remain our little secret.'

'A confession, Bishop?'

'Confession to a non-Catholic is indeed a humiliation. To a Catholic, Thomas, it holds out the possibility of absolution.'

'And the memory of sin? Can anyone absolve that?'

'We try, Thomas. We try.'

CHAPTER 6

I do not drive a Mercedes, nor do I drive a Volkswagen. I drive an English car. Other than the Volkswagen which, I'm told, is assembled in Dublin – the first non-German franchise – few cars are manufactured in Ireland. Even in daylight the scenery in this part of Ireland does not obtrude. I am not dragged unwillingly by dramatic beauty into the world about me. This is not a colourful county. Fierce colour in Ireland is most often found in language. I, of course, am content not to be ravished. September is here. It is cold and it is wet. They do not have Indian summers in Ireland. They do not normally have summers at all. This year's sudden summer days were an aberration.

There are few cars on the road. It is an under-populated country. This fact, whether demonstrated by the comparatively empty roads or by the nation's difficulty in creating a successful modern economy due to its small population, which becomes each year ever smaller, inevitably leads one in any conversation, however short, to the tragedy of emigration. Which leads to the tragedy of the Famine and its cruel mathematics. Subtly in the mind of the listener the shadow of guilt arises, unjustified yet somehow essential if the conversation is to continue.

I am a careful driver. Harriet is not. This thought comes each time I drive. It is a connection to her that I need. I remind myself almost daily of my dependence. How else is my life – this shadow life without her – to be lived? Harriet. Dear Harriet. Not dear Harriet. When I first saw you, you were wearing white. Remember? You wore dresses then. I remember the dress you wore that first day. How easy it was. My terrible, easy first time. It should have been just that.

I turn slowly into the main street and approach the market square, which is used as an unofficial car park by the town. I succumbed some time ago to the *amour-propre* of the few I know here and no longer refer to this place as a village. As I manoeuvre my car into a space close to the library entrance, a task that is less than challenging since there are only four other cars, someone shouts. Then screams. And Olivia O'Hara, her head buried in a book, steps straight out in front of me, sways slightly and seems to disappear, while still holding her book, beneath the wheels of my car. My foot and the brake are in violent collision, my wrist twists to kill the ignition. I almost fall out of my car. People are running across the road. Olivia O'Hara is lying on her side facing the wheels, her arms outstretched towards them like a lover. She is still. Then she rolls over onto her back and looks up at me.

'Oh God! It's the German! You nearly knocked me down, Mr Middlehoff. Indeed you did knock me down. You nearly killed me.'

I lean over her and with another man whom I recognise as Mr Brannigan help her to her feet. Her face is slightly grazed and blood from her knee seeps through her woollen stockings.

'I'll drive her to the hospital. My car's just here.'

Mr Brannigan wears a long, heavy raincoat and leans slightly on his furled umbrella, as though his height embarrassed him and he wished to shrink a little. He speaks with the fast rhythms of a man from Cork, an accent with which Bridget has made me familiar. It is one she mocks and mimics.

'I don't think a hospital is necessary. Dr Carter is just two doors away.'

They look at me, the German speaking with authority. They look at me in silence. Dr Carter's name resonates with the memory of another O'Hara child.

'Oh Mr Middlehoff . . .'

The sound of Olivia O'Hara's voice redeems us from remembered and imagined fears.

'I mustn't forget my books. I ordered them specially.'

She looks around in panic. The shocked victim always seeks the insignificant, as a reassurance of normality. Looking at her it is clear she may cry at any moment. Crying is not weeping. I know that all will be well.

'Do not worry Miss O'Hara, I will retrieve the books.'

I pick them up. *Eugénie Grandet*, François Mauriac's *Thérèse Desqueyroux*. I am surprised this last is available in the local library. Perhaps Mauriac's Catholicism? Perhaps respect for his Nobel Prize, or his passion for the mysteries of sin and redemption?

'I'm going through a bit of a French phase. I think it's a bit like Ireland, only more sophisticated.'

She smiles. And I am reassured. Her smile, I note, is a little crooked, and reminiscent of that of Harriet. Then she hobbles, supported by both Mr Brannigan and myself. This way will be quicker than by car, and the manoeuvres involved in seating her in either my car or that of Mr Brannigan might prove even more painful.

Susan Carter opens the door. Her husband rarely speaks of her, whether through a natural reticence in personal matters or through boredom. I remember a comment about her love of hunting. I remember because of Harriet's passion for the same violent sport, which women often undertake more recklessly than men. 'Susan's only connection with this country is hunting,' he'd said once. I know this kind of Englishwoman. Their education is equestrian. A hierarchical journey from Pony Club to the hunt that ensures an inculcation of courage and will. Physical courage is strangely compelling in a woman. When I said that to Robert Carter one evening he'd replied with some bitterness, 'Susan required more than physical courage to marry me, an older ex-Major. War-damaged, as her mother put it to me once during an uncomfortable meeting.' After which outburst the subject of Susan had remained closed. In a rare personal moment he told me he'd left Britain for a country without constant reminders of the men he would not see again. He is good looking in that Battle of Britain boyish way, about which I feel no animosity. His appearance will not change greatly with age – his handsomeness will simply fade. As Susan's flat looks will fade as she too becomes middle-aged in about a decade or so, as the luminosity of blondness drains gently away.

'Robert!' she calls out in a high, almost childish voice. Then, turning to us, 'I'm sorry, we were having lunch.'

Why should she be sorry? The English of a certain class seem to live in a permanent state of apology.

'Miss O'Hara.'

He walks towards her unhurriedly.

'Please don't call me Miss. Reminds me of school.'

We follow her into his surgery and help her on to his examining table.

'Will you turn around while I try to get my stockings down.'

89

'That might be painful, Miss O'Hara. Let me soak the area first. And then I will pull the curtain.'

'Don't ruin them.' And she tries to smile. 'Will someone go and tell my Dada where I am? He can tell Mama better than I can. Don't tell him on the phone. It's too much. Mama, well she's not ready for any shocks, even small ones. He's up at the showroom, trying to sell a car or a tractor, I can't remember. Just get to him before anyone tells her.'

She speaks urgently, as though the breaking of the news of this thankfully minor incident is more important than any pain she might be suffering. She is too young to be so protective.

'I will take Miss O'Hara home. I have no further appointments this afternoon.'

'Thank you Dr Carter. Please stop calling me Miss. You make me grown in a way I don't want to be with this Miss O'Hara business.'

'Very well. It's Olivia, then.' He motions us to leave. Outside the surgery door Mr Brannigan starts to tremble.

'I can't do this. I'm a bit shaky, you know. They talk about me I'm sure, even to you, Mr Middlehoff.'

'No they do not, Mr Brannigan.'

'Ah well, then you really are a stranger. I know there's whispering. Tom O'Hara, well he steps in sometimes, into strange situations. We never acknowledge it after an incident. He always goes back to being just a decent neighbour. It helps to keep things normal. So if I go to tell him we might be forced to talk. And silence is best.'

He is now gripping his umbrella as if to stop the shaking of his hands.

'Very well. I will tell Mr O'Hara.'

'Thank you. You must think me a coward. After all, I am a neighbour and, I suppose, a family friend.' He hesitates. 'It's awful to ask you to do it. I know it's small thing, this incident. I mean, Olivia's barely scratched, but with the history . . .'

We walk to our cars. We nod to each other and part. I drive slowly, trying to prepare myself to tell Tom O'Hara that I have injured his daughter. He takes the news calmly. Just stands there. Rooted. This man strikes me as one who grew slowly, like an oak tree, and will withstand much.

'It's nothing, you say?'

'Her face – slightly grazed. Some bruising on the knee. I don't know. She's shaken, that's all. Dr Carter will drive her home. You've had a shock, Mr O'Hara. Would you like me to drive you to your house?'

'No. But thank you. I'm going to walk. It's not far and this town knows not to face Sissy in her den. Her grief terrifies them and I don't blame them. No one will tell her. Besides, the walk will give me time to think of what to say to Sissy. Though I'll walk quickly enough. No loitering.'

Then as he starts to walk away, he turns suddenly and asks, 'Have you thought about the gate? I've heard nothing from you.'

'Yes. I have thought about it, Mr O'Hara.' I pause.

'No decision though? A slow man, are you, Mr Middlehoff? A bit like myself. Sissy's the quick one. Though I fell for her in an instant. She was like a bolt of lightning in my life. Anyway, sure it's your gate. Ah well . . . goodbye Mr Middlehoff.'

'Please call me Thomas.'

'You know, I think I won't. I don't think we'll ever be close enough for that.'

And I can sense, as he walks down the street, the need in him to hurry and his resistance to it as though his heavy body is a force-field against which he needs to do battle. I go to my car and turn towards home. I had brought a message to a man who must now tell the tale. He must face his task.

When I get home Bridget tells me that the Garda have been fully informed by Dr Carter who wants me to ring him, and that a Garda will come to Lake House tomorrow.

'I'm glad it's nothing – but that Olivia O'Hara! She's always got her head in a book that girl. She starts reading them as she walks out of the library. It's almost happened before and she should be more careful after . . . the tragedy.' And her voice trails away.

'Miss O'Hara was in no way to blame.'

Bridget turns to leave; she is clearly rather distressed. Fear for the O'Haras, possibly.

'And Mr Middlehoff, I nearly banged myself

again on that table you have in the hall! That table is all angles. It's dangerous. A child could brain itself on it. It's my opinion, Mr Middlehoff, that marble should only be seen in church. That's what I think.'

'There are no children in this house.'

'You're right there, Mr Middlehoff. And wrong.'

And she set off to the kitchen promising – no, insisting on – tea. I need it, she tells me. And today I say yes. She is pleased.

'Cake?' Why not please her further?

'Yes. Thank you Bridget.'

I ring Robert Carter.

'Robert, forgive me for today's intrusion. You were the closest – again. She's all right?'

'All thankfully minor. Dr Sullivan will take over now – the dressing on her knee needs to be changed, then a few days' rest . . . I was glad to be of help. I rather like that girl. She was splendid at the inquest.'

'What did you think of it – the inquest?'

'We are outsiders. There was much to consider here . . . However, I think the coroner did his job with due consideration to the feelings of all concerned. He might have been a little harder on the chemist who supplied the chemicals. Still, the poor man was almost hysterical with grief. However, I still feel that there was nothing sinister. Though I gather there are rumours, but it is my opinion that most people agree that the matter is now, quite correctly, closed.'

'I agree. We are outsiders. Will you thank Susan for me, Robert. She was most kind.'

'She is.'

Robert Carter's conversational style is one with which I feel at ease. He uses language to mark distance in a neutral zone. We recognise a certain similarity in our verbal style. Thus we are aware that this conversation is over and thus our friendship continues.

CHAPTER 7

Some days later I visit the O'Haras. In another country I would take flowers, but here it might be misconstrued. Propriety rules. Instead I take books as a gift. Goethe's *Elective Affinities* and Fontane's *Effi Briest*. Though I do not know Olivia O'Hara well, I feel an affinity and a sympathy towards her. Nothing more. And since she has been wounded, doubly wounded, I wish to warn her of other dangers.

It is Sunday and the previous day I had asked Mr O'Hara if a visit was acceptable. Reluctantly he'd agreed. Perhaps he believed I would talk about the gate. He was wrong.

Their house is long and low. It is a bungalow, but one built about fifty years ago and has a charm that is altogether lacking in the new concrete prairie buildings now scattered through the fields of Ireland. What Harriet refers to as bungalow hell. I stand outside this unlucky house, as its owner calls it, press the bell and to my surprise Olivia O'Hara opens the door.

★   ★   ★

'Hello Mr Middlehoff. Don't look surprised: I'm fine now. I hobble a bit but Dada tells me it looks romantic. Come in. We're in here.'

I follow her into their sitting room. It is large and dark. Heavy red velvet curtains obscure daylight and the silence I noted when I entered the hall permeates this room also, like a curtain one dare not draw. I stand awkwardly, waiting for a way into what I know is the formless darkness in which they move and from which I now understand I cannot escape for some time. I regret considerably that I did not post my books to Olivia O'Hara. Indeed, as I survey the scene I regret knowing them at all.

'Mama, Mr Middlehoff is here.'

'Mrs O'Hara.'

She is sitting quite upright in a large armchair. She is composed. She is dressed in a black skirt and a black high-buttoned cardigan. When she looks at me her face is drained of expression. True nothingness. True grief. Tom O'Hara follows me into their sitting room and with him comes a feeling of a sudden normality.

'Now, Mr Middlehoff, you will have some sherry?'

And from the handsome mahogany sideboard with its silver teapots and trays and goblets he pours me a drink I loathe. Dry for me and sweet for Mrs O'Hara. For Olivia he squirts soda water into a tumbler. She has, he tells me, taken the pledge. I look confused . . . And the promise made by the youth of Ireland to abstain from drink as part of a temperance movement is explained to me. The banal, I believe, is now expected of me conversationally and I obey.

'Dr Carter tells me that there are no problems with your knee.'

I have failed. At the name Dr Carter I see Mrs O'Hara jerk her head slightly, as though I'd inadvertently brushed my hand against her face. She recovers. I am a guest. These are a courteous people. Again the silence settles. Then, suddenly, music from another room. Had it been machine-gun fire all three of them could not have looked more horrified.

'My God! What is that? What is that, Tom? Music? It's music!'

I feel that I am frozen in a painting of this family and the now-closed eyes of father and daughter tell an enigmatic story. The viewer would never know that the closed eyes are a reaction to an assault of a music that they cannot hear. Then their eyes open and a weary Tom O'Hara smiles sadly at his wife.

'It's Daragh. He's got the wireless on. It's coming from his room.'

Olivia jumps up from her chair. She winces slightly as she rushes towards the door.

'I'm sorry Mr Middlehoff. Will you excuse me?'

I stand up as she leaves the room. I wish that I too could leave but Mrs O'Hara is now speaking rapidly.

'How can that happen Tom? How I can hear music in this house? Music? Music in this house?'

'It's his wireless.'

'He has his own wireless?'

'Yes, he has.'

'How?'

'I got it for him. I told him only to play it when you were out. He needs something. He enjoys Radio Luxembourg.'

'Radio Luxembourg? He needs Radio Luxembourg? Now, in the days . . . ?'

'He's young, Sissy.'

'So is Olivia. She just reads her books quietly.'

'Ah, Sissy, he's three years younger than Olivia and whatever age he gets to be, reading will not be what comforts him. He's a boy.'

'But . . . he . . . He loved books. He was like Olivia. Like me. Like you.'

'The two boys listened to Radio Luxembourg. You know that, Sissy. He didn't only read books. He was wild as well. You know that. Climbing up on the roof. Diving too deep, roller skating too fast. Daragh's wild in his own way – but he's a different boy, he's a different child. Now, Sissy darling, don't get so upset angel. Think of our poor visitor. He came in from Lake House to give Olivia a present.'

'Ask Daragh to stop! I'm sorry Tom, I can't bear it. I'm sorry, Mr Middlehoff. I can't bear it.'

I understand that at least. And I understand that she will have to bear it. I feel I must say something, anything.

'I understand, Mrs O'Hara.'

'I doubt that, Mr Middlehoff. Forgive me I'm . . . I'm . . .'

What do I have to lose? I say the words quickly: 'You are ill, Mrs O'Hara. You are seriously ill with grief.'

She looks down at her hands and slowly twists the rings on her wedding finger. A Victorian sapphire ring and a wedding ring. Then she looks up at me.

'You're right Mr Middlehoff. I am indeed ill with grief. And I know it. But they don't. They refuse to accept that I am ill.' And she looks defiantly at her husband.

'Ah Sissy, we must not do this to Mr Middlehoff.'

'Please, Mr O'Hara. I am full of sympathy.'

And just then the music stops. Mrs O'Hara closes her eyes.

'Would you like another sherry, Mr Middlehoff?'

'No. Thank you. I wanted to bring a small gift – these books – to Olivia. I will leave them for her.'

'No, please wait. She'll be back in a second. Ah, here she is. Thank you darling. He didn't . . . ?'

'No Dada, he was grand about it.'

She looks at me and bites her lip. I am selfish, and even was I kinder what could I do? What could I say? I wish to leave. I hand the books to her.

'Thank you Mr Middlehoff. Goethe! I think he's on the banned list.'

'Olivia is working her way through it!' And Tom O'Hara laughs. 'With regard to books I trust her. We've had Father Dwyer down here before and she always argues him out of his worries.'

There exists between this father and daughter what rarely exists between parent and child: moral trust. Trust. My father felt the same about me. Once. When he saw me as a teenager reading Gottfried Benn's *Morgue*. But that was long ago. I rise to leave. They press me to stay. To have another sherry. But I know that they too wish for the end of this visit. Tragedy has savagely dislocated them from their lives, from the normal rhythms in their house and they need to establish a pattern for a new life, in private. I have intruded. And will not again. I say goodbye with a small bow to Mrs O'Hara, who looks straight into my eyes for a disturbing second and then turns away.

'I'll show you to the door.'

'Thank you.'

And Olivia walks, still limping slightly, out into the cold and towards my car as I protest.

'Please stay inside. It really is too cold.'

'No, it's good for me to be outside . . .'

'When do you return to school?'

'The middle of the week after next. They've let me come back late.'

'After this year you will attend university?'

'No.'

She has that quality of certainty, which Harriet also has.

'No?'

'When I'm finished at school I think I should stay at home for some time. I talked to my father.'

'That seems such a pity.'

'Does it? It doesn't seem such a pity to me. Something is telling me to hold the fort. We're all wounded. It's going to take a long time to heal us. I'd feel I was leaving a battle scene. Leaving them to cope alone. I don't want to be away from here. I have made my mind up: this is where I stay for a while. They both need me. Mama must survive otherwise they'll both . . . be lost, I think. My father is blind and deaf and dumb with love. Yeats. Mrs Garvey thinks the man has ruined us.'

'Miss O'Hara. Olivia. May I call you Olivia?'

'Well I'm too young for you to keep calling me Miss O'Hara. You and Dr Carter are trying to make me older than I am. But up until last year I wore ankle socks at school.' She laughs. 'I'm sure a German girl wouldn't be wearing ankle socks at sixteen.'

And I think, in this country young women of seventeen are indeed young, much younger than their equivalent in Germany, even before the war drowned our all youth.

'Olivia. I do not seek to interfere but this is a major decision. One with consequences. You would be wrong to let this chance – this time in your life – slip away.'

'Wrong, Mr Middlehoff? No. I don't think so. I have a duty and I don't feel the same about my life.

101

I am less wrapped up in it. Anyway, as the nuns say, people wrapped up in themselves make very small parcels. I'm not ambitious any more. You see, I think with his future gone I should wait a bit longer for my own. I want to be in this place to let it stay with me longer. To let him stay with me longer.'

'You must miss him all the time.'

'No, I don't.'

'I do not understand you.'

'You see, Mr Middlehoff, I keep him here with me. He's with me all the time. Here. In this house. So no, I don't miss him at all: I'm living in the house with him. That's my decision. It's not lonely. And I talk to him, silently. We have things to work out together. About what I did. The choice I made that day, that moment twist-turning on the porch. Maybe we'll have to agree I did the wrong thing, took the wrong turning. Decided – no, gambled – that I had time to make it up to him after we'd saved my mother. I can't quite make out what he thinks yet.'

I am inexpressibly moved. And worried for her. What can I say to her?

'I shouldn't have told you. Ah, here's Dada. Don't tell him what I said.'

'I am sorry, Mr Middlehoff. I should have realised it would be a mistake for you to visit. We are having a hard battle here, aren't we Olivia?'

'We are, Dada.'

'It would seem as though your wife is ill still with the shock.'

'I hope so. In my bleaker moments I think she's dying on me. People can simply cease to live. You must know that.'

'She went missing yesterday,' Olivia interjects quickly.

'But you found her, obviously.'

'Oh yes.'

'Where had she gone?'

'She hadn't gone anywhere! Had she, Dada? Not really. She just wasn't where we thought she should be.'

'She'd done an unexpected thing.'

'Yes. But we don't want unexpected things any more.'

'No.'

'I panicked. When Olivia told me, I panicked. Came running down from work and my face must have told a story because when she saw me Olivia started crying, "Oh Dada, Dada, we'll find her. We must find her for you." Didn't you, darling?'

I noted she had not said she would try to find her mother for herself.

'We were frantic with terror that we'd lose her. We rang the hospital and we went everywhere, the cathedral, the graveyard, down the canal walk. No sign of her. And when we got back, there she was in the kitchen! Laughing! It was awful. "Where were you?" we cried. "I'm a prisoner, am I?" Can you imagine? This is Sissy talking. But it's not our Sissy. That's not her. But she went on, defiantly, and said, "I met a friend. He was passing through

103

the town. Bumped into him. We went for a drink in the Dublin Arms. What's wrong with that? Can't I do that? Am I trapped in my house?" We just sat there listening to this stranger talking to us. Praying we'd see Sissy, even sad, sad Sissy, again. Then suddenly everything was back to normal. Well the new normal, with just the fear. We're disconnected from everything. There's just the four of us. Lost.'

I feel suffocated by their pain. It is too close. A witness needs distance. I feel I am being forced into a false intimacy. Standing there beside them I have no hiding place. Yet decency requires some gesture from me. I must say something, if only to leave with some grace. About the gate perhaps. But I am too late.

'Dada's right, we think she's dying on us. She doesn't eat. She just sits there and goes back into that silent world. She's gone down to nothing. Her black suit is hanging off her and all she'll wear is that, or one of the black cardigans and skirts she's wearing today. She's rolling up the waistbands of her skirts to make them stay on. I offered to move the buttons and she turned on me: how useless I am at sewing and stuff. And then she was sorry. But her "sorry" was so far away. Like she is now. So far away.'

I know this disconnection. And that it rarely passes. I remain silent.

'It's not getting any better. Sometimes I think it's worse. She's not alive in the normal sense.'

And I wonder what is the normal sense of being alive? Am I alive in the normal sense, living with so much of me missing?

'What is awful is when she just sits there watching Daragh going to school each day. She just watches him. He runs from the house to get away from her . . . from us.'

And I think he'll be running away for years.

'Olivia does the opposite, don't you darling? I don't know which is best. I made Sissy stay here. Living close to what is lost – do you remember, Mr Middlchoff? Does anything work?'

'I do not know. If I could tell you, Mr O'Hara, I would. However, I must go now. I have written to my father about the gate, Mr O'Hara. It originally came from the house of his childhood, you see.'

My lie appals me. He looks at me hard. He knows the subject has been changed and is for a second not certain how to react.

'I will contact you as soon as I have a reply. It is fair to warn you that my father rarely makes sudden decisions.'

'Sudden decisions are usually made for us, Mr Middlehoff. I'm sorry. I've blundered into your family history. Blind, I suppose, not knowing which way to go or what to do for him now that I can do nothing. I honestly didn't know I'd asked for a family heirloom. I'll put the idea out of my mind now. It was a mad thought. I was a bit mad at the time.'

I am aware that I may have broken the connection between us. I hadn't wished to do that quite so harshly. However, equally I do not wish to come any closer to the O'Haras. The agony of others obscures rather than clarifies. The Greeks were right to keep the great events off stage. Send the information by messenger. Essential, if only because there is always the possibility that the messenger may be wrong.

CHAPTER 8

. . . this young man is talking to me. This young man wants me to talk to him. Everybody wants me, Sissy O'Hara, to talk to them. It will be a triumph for them. 'Sissy talked to me,' they'll say. 'Chatted away, just like old times.' If we talk in this country we're all right. Silence is death to us. And that's why my silence frightens them. Let them be frightened! I'm sorry. Let them be frightened. I don't want to make the sound words make any more. Not me, say I. Not me.

'Mrs O'Hara? Mrs O'Hara! Talk to me, Mrs O'Hara. We've been sitting here a while now Mrs O'Hara.'

We have indeed. And why not sit in silence? Why not live in silence? The Cistercians do. They look radiant. Maybe they've got all the answers, since they never ask a question. So you, Brendan Begley, sitting opposite me here, do not ask me for the sound of words. Everyone is hungry for the sound of the word, for the fare of life. We feel we'll starve without it. And we fear starvation. But I am not hungry. Not for human sound nor for those who make it. I am not hungry for people. Neither the sight nor the sound of them. I am hungry for nothing except what I cannot have. I will starve within and without, without him. What is it that they want from me when they say 'Sissy, you have other children? Should I feed on them? No. And so I eat less and less. They are all worried about me. They think I'm dying. Tom thinks I'm dying. Dying? I'm dead! In the week before Tom finally relented and let me come here he tried one last time to love me back to life. Love! He has such faith in love! He is love! He believes that he can make it course through me – a circulation of love pumping from his heart into my heart – pushing through the veins, pumping and pushing that old rhythm that brought life into the world. He thinks love, his love, can bring me back to life. A man in love never gives up. Never. Tom O'Hara is certain he will not fail in this. And he knows that if he fails in this he is lost. And I know that. I am what he has to show for life. I am all he has to show for life; that his love for me triumphed and the children who followed. Two of them gone . . .

And still I could not join him. He was holding his heart out to me. There you are, Sissy. Take it. Partake of it. This is my body. The way the Sacred Heart cries out to us in that picture in the kitchen. What a picture in a kitchen! You'll see His Sacred Heart bleeding in bedrooms and kitchens all over Ireland. But never in sitting rooms, or in none that I've seen. No, sitting rooms are for mahogany sideboards and sherry and sherry glasses, Waterford glasses, cut as though by a dentist's drill into so many peaks of sharpness it's a wonder we've ever had the courage to touch them. And Irish linen napkins, huge with heavy folds you could almost hide an infant in. Polished wood and crystal clarity and white napkins, order, perfect order in sitting rooms and in convent parlours and bleeding hearts in kitchens.

And he brought his bleeding heart to me, and all the bulk of his man's body towards me like a gift. It's what women want, they say, heart and body, and I was still frozen, looking at him with nothing, no light or warmth glimmering in my face. Nothing. I gave him nothing. I left him lying there with his heart in his hand. He could be lying there for eternity. The place I'm in is the place I will stay. It is not a place for Tom. It has no place for him. I do not want him here. And never will again. And that's the truth. I do not want Tom here. I'm waiting for someone else. Someone I have not seen in many months. Someone I will never see again. My son is dead. There can be no doubt about it. None at all. I have left Tom and Olivia and Daragh. They must be lonely, I suppose. But I can't help them now.

So I have gone down somewhere, to a place without a name. Maybe some day an explorer will find it and will map it out. Is it an island I'm on? How did I get here? Was the crossing rough? And this hidden place on the island: how did I find it? Were there twists and turns? Did I stumble?

Or was I thrown down here? Maybe I'll be the one to map it, to write the directions and then, with all my late-come cruelty, I'll put up a sign that says 'KEEP OUT'. Stay out Tom! Stay out! Stay with those who live, Tom.

We separated from each other even before I came into this hospital. The first separation of our souls. That's a deep separation. We two who lived so peacefully in one another's souls and whose bodies slept so peacefully together night after night. No separation except to have my children, and then home after days to the shape of the night, which was his shape. Shaping the hours and shaping me into the morning when I would disentangle and wait for nightfall again. But that's over now. I would not respond. And that is separation. It lies in the turning away, in the blank look that says, I do not recognise you any more. Are you, you? Are you? Were you my lovely husband? And who are you now? Tell me. Who are you now? Ah. That is separation. Leaving a man with all the history of the words that worked, and the stroking that worked, the union that worked, leaving him with all the things he learned in all that life of love amounting to nothing, nothing. Nothing working any more.

It was sad to listen to him. He was whispering because we always whispered in bed, even before the children came. Why? I don't remember. The children took longer to come to me than I'd imagined, but they came. I always told Mrs Garvey, 'they are waiting for you May. When they're ready they will come.' And one of them is clearly ready. Someone told me May Garvey is pregnant again. She kept it secret until she was past the danger time. Didn't tell me. Kind, that was kind. And this time she is certain they say that he or she will make it to the gate of life and push it open and tumble into life, screaming. And his or her mother will be laughing. Wildly.

I remember the wild laughter after Olivia. Laughter that was even wilder after . . . after. They say it doesn't matter whether it's a boy or a girl. It does, though. You're looking for yourself in a girl and with a boy it's all a-wonder. It's all a-wonder. Fathers and daughters, is that all a-wonder? Not with Tom. They're great friends, Tom and Olivia. I was never 'friends' with my boys. No. And Daragh? Mysterious child. I can't think at all about my other daughter. Silent I remain. As did she. But all a-wonder? No. Tom is all a-wonder with me. Only with me. He lay whispering last night. Last night? No, sure wasn't I in here last night and the night before and before? What day is it now? What night was it then? Anyway, what-ever night it was, he tried again. After we'd been lying there, me frozen even underneath all those blankets and eiderdowns, he said, 'Sissy, listen to me. Come over to me Sissy, like you used to.' I lay there and I whispered, less than a whisper – the sound was like a leaf falling, because I thought it would hurt him less if he could barely

hear me. 'I can't, Tom. I can't.' And then his slow-
sighing, 'All right darling,' and me, trying to save
him with a little bit of energy still left for him,
whispered again, 'Give up on me, Tom. Let me
drift away.' And his 'No Sissy. We started out on
a road and we're going on together. Remember
that little advertisement, the two children in their
Start-rite shoes walking hand in hand that I
framed for you years ago? Is it in the attic now?'
I was so tired but I made a bit of an effort, for
old times' sake. 'I don't know where it is Tom.' I
did. I'd hidden it. I didn't want to remember what
had been waiting down the road for us. I never
knew how he managed to get a copy of the original advertisement, God knows where. But he had
it framed and I kept it on my dressing table, and
when I used to put my lipstick on each day I'd
think, there you are, Sissy! Armed for the fray,
and I'd pat the picture. The Start-rite kids. The
children holding hands with the long road before
them. Why did it mean so much to us? Is it all
just the memory of childhood dreams?

I can't think of those things any more, or of
the weariness of carrying all this love from him.
It's heavy, his love. He just won't take it away. It's
tiring me out. All his love. And his voice comes
back, 'Sissy, travelling down the road with you was
all I have ever wanted in life. And I'll tell you
something else, that's all there is in life. It is the
greatest thing in life. The glory of it Sissy! The
beauty of it. So no matter how long this takes, I'll

wait. I'll wait for the slightest sign from you and then I'll wait for the sign after and then I'll make you laugh a few times and I'll bring you a pair of shoes from Dublin or a pale blue silk scarf or a new twinset. Blue's your colour. Miss Coyle will help me with the shade. I'll wait, because I know you won't wear it for a while because colour will hurt you. But one day you will wear it and I'll be there waiting for you to look at me again, really look at me. And I'll wait for the day you walk head-high up the road and I'll notice that your feet lift a little and I'll know that within maybe a year or so you'll walk the way you once did. So gracefully, Sissy. I loved to walk beside you. You'll go back to your lipstick and I'll buy you a gold compact, old and beautiful. I'll search in those little shops in Dublin where secret histories are wrapped up in little velvet envelopes and I'll be drawn to the right one, the one owned by a woman who was loved day and night, night and day by a man who couldn't believe that he had walking beside him the treasure of all the world. Oh I'll wait, Sissy.'

Indeed you will, Tom. Poor Tom, you'll always wait for me. But I'm gone Tom, I'm gone. Then I thought, try to help him Sissy. For old times' sake. Haul yourself up through all these layers of silence, which press on me down here in this place that I stay in now. It's a hidden, animal place. Try, Sissy. Try, for old times' sake. I did. You can give me that. I found a few words: 'I'm lying here,

Tom, listening to the loveliness of all this but it's as though the words are just wisps of poetry that I don't understand. I'm so sorry but I can't love anything.' Oh, but he would not stop. Love-lines pouring out of him. Until I had to say again, a bit louder this time, 'Stop loving me! I'm too tired for love.' 'You're full of love Sissy. It's just frozen at the moment. I think it's to protect you. Even to feel a little love now would hurt too much. You're all bruised by love and by the absence of who you loved. That's what it is, a constant absence. He's missing.' I couldn't stand it. I shouted at him: 'But he's missing in the house. *In the house, Tom! Do you understand? In the house!*' I could hear Tom crying beside me. What else could he do? What else could I do? Nothing.

After a long time he whispered, 'We'll walk around the house Sissy, in and out of bedrooms, and we'll find him again one day, the easier memories.' 'It's his absence we'll find. That's all, Tom.' 'Well Sissy, if that's all, maybe absence has its own power. Maybe you can snuggle an absence down in you. Honour it. Love it. Come on, Sissy. Come for a walk with me around the house. Let me take your hand my lovely love, we'll walk around this house in a dream . . . into every room and tell each other how it is that we remember him . . . look, the door of our bedroom . . . remember how he'd peer in, such a skinny, sunny lad, a bit too soft for his own good, and then he'd go scuttling back to his own room.'

114

And then I did an heroic thing. I took his hand and walked around our kingdom and he was my guide. It was all a dream. What did it matter? It was a dream walk, hand in hand, Tom and me, in the bed where we made them. 'And look there, in the hall, where he slipped on the wet tiles and broke his arm. Come to the kitchen, do you remember him sitting there mushing up the jelly and the ice cream into a raspberry or orange-coloured mess, grinning all over his face? Ah well. Do I see some comics and a few *Reader's Digests?* Do you remember the way he'd cut things from the *Reader's Digest* to give to Mrs Garvey to help her about the babies? He was a bit sweet on Mrs Garvey; they had a bit of an understanding. Isn't it strange, the people with whom that little bit of love happens? Nothing grand or great, just a little bit of love. Recognition. There was something hurt in him as well, like Mrs Garvey. Maybe the asthma. That might have been it. Not able to run. No, able to run but not allowed, that's different. But he did all right at the swimming. I wondered at that. I often wonder, Sissy, was he all that happy at school? Strange to ask that now. We thought we'd years ahead to talk to him. Years and years. It's a mistake we all make, Sissy. We wouldn't be able for life otherwise.' And I thought, I'm not able for it Tom. Nor will I ever be able again. The broken perfection of my boy, part of him missing, lies out there in the graveyard. And all of him is missing here in this house. Here in my life. And I whispered to Tom, 'All of him is missing as I lie here, waiting, waiting.' 'Let's love just the memory, Sissy. Like they say, in loving memory.'

And he cradled me and at last I let him. Poor Tom. Then he took my hands to his lips and kissed each long bony finger. My hands don't belong to me at all. I am a round woman. Then Tom opened the top buttons of my nightdress and found first one and then the other breast and stroked them too, and I suppose he began to hope. And his hands moved to stroke my legs and then my thighs and . . . And for a moment I felt the pity of it all, but I just couldn't come out of this place I am in. I just couldn't. 'I can't. I can't. Oh Tom, I just can't.' And oh Lord that man, that lovely man, just said, as though he were, like Christ, the very embodiment of love, 'It's all right Sissy. I will just keep on loving and stroking and waiting. Down however many years it takes, I'm going to bring you back to love, which is life, Sissy. I can do it. I can do it.'

So here I am in this mental hospital. I am not afraid to say these words. But only to myself.

'Mrs O'Hara! Mrs O'Hara!'

The young man is calling out to me again. I know this young man. Known him for years. He's trying to talk to me by talking to me. Trying to break into me and pull out words. To show them, like a miracle, 'Behold her! Listen to her! She speaks! Sissy speaks!' No. No miracles today, Brendan. I look around me. Why? I have no interest in where I am. But I am – still. And I suppose I must be placed somewhere. So they have placed me in this room. I did not protest. Why should I? I am in a little consulting room – looks like a sitting room really – in the hospital. There are no mahogany tables. No crystal either. Too dangerous. This is a bleeding-heart sitting room without the picture. Still it's cheerful enough, with a view of a high cypress hedge that almost hides the stone wall. Mental hospitals need to be careful, I suppose. Walls are built for different reasons. Who'd break into a mental hospital, and I never heard of anyone breaking out of this one. Though I suppose it must happen. I won't be the first. I want to be here. I came here. Olivia is angry with me. She is ashamed, I think.

'Mrs O'Hara? Did you hear what I was saying?'

I wonder why he's calling me Mrs O'Hara in that tone? He used to steal the apples from the back garden. He knows who I used to be. Sissy O'Hara. 'The Lady', as they used to call me. Who was she? Mrs O'Hara? I was always quiet with the hidden thing within me. The knowledge that no woman on earth was more loved than me. That I could guide and protect my children and keep my house and live love all the time. Live love. Just that. What woman would let anyone in on such a secret? It would be too unfair. And when life got so tough for Tom, was that my fault? I had to have him near me when, oh God, when I fought that long battle for my daughter. He closed that business that he had and did as I asked. He was on call for me and my fear. 'Don't be further than five minutes from me Tom. In case she . . .' Yes. Five minutes. I insisted. We should have moved to another town then and I'd not have been destroyed by this second death.

'Mrs O'Hara? . . . Sissy?'

He can't make up his mind, poor boy. Is it Mrs O'Hara or Sissy?

'You wanted to come in. It's such a good sign.'

I'm here because of pain, I want to say to him. The pain beyond feeling. Pain so bad the only place I wanted to be was in hospital. I'm hoping you can control the pain because perhaps the only thing to finish it is death. I want death. Often it washes over me like a benediction, I want death. A sin. Despair? Is that my sin? But God seems determined to take His time, and His terms are tough. You can't end it by yourself. You have to wait till He decides to put you out of your misery. Gives you some disease or, if He's kind, a heart attack to rip the life out of you by tearing the heart to pieces. Well it's shredded as far as I'm concerned but it keeps on stubbornly beating.

'I think you're doing this for Tom and the children.'

Did he need training for this? This child? Let me think. He can't be much more than thirty.

Brendan Begley. A doctor now. They tell me he'll be a Mr in the future, a consultant. Brilliant. Suddenly I want to wound him and ask him, are you happy with Mary? Mary Dougherty, whose father owns a factory in Killucan and who was a good match for you. I can always spot the good-match brigade. You can see it in their faces. Sometimes in as little as a year. The price was too high. Yes, you can see it in their faces. Faster in the girls though – the ones who marry the older man with land. You can see the fear, after a time, that the age is infecting them as well. And sometimes, later, that shiver-sliver of disgust. Brendan Begley's is a boy's story. And he got it wrong. He should have married Sorcha O'Leary. Broke her heart. She went off to Dublin. To hide her pain-shame. Brendan was too careful. Thought a farmer's daughter wasn't quite good enough. The farm too small. And so he married Mary Dougherty.

Why are these nothing things coming back to me? Because they're bits of rubbish on the surface of a mind. How does he feel about Sorcha now? Who married here in the cathedral a couple of years ago? To her mother's great satisfaction. Sorcha, the rejected one, snapped up by the son of one of Ireland's richest men. Well done Sorcha! You loved this good-looking boy, tall and dark and Irish-handsome. I'll give Brendan that, he's the kind of boy a girl could break her heart over. And did. But you recovered, didn't you Sorcha? Yes,

Sorcha went on and made a life, as they say. Like making a bed. So that children can fall out of it. 'She's done well for herself,' that's what they say. Well if you miss first prize, the love of your life, doing well for yourself is a decent second.

Must be pretty galling for Brendan, though, as he gets into bed night after night with the wrong woman. Thinking of another. Not of Mary, his wife. Is she any comfort, Brendan? Oh she's nice enough. Pretty as well. I remember her as a child. The little corkscrew curls and the pale skin. But Sorcha's swishing-around wildness you could almost touch! Sorcha was yours, Brendan. I could see that. We could all see that. I remember I saw the two of you walking up the town once on a snow-cold morning. You were about seventeen, eighteen maybe. Laughing, laughing, flashing magnificence at us all. So I thought, get out of their way. Let their magnificence shine out. The sudden shine-out magnificence of life and love on that frozen day, and your eyes, Brendan, flashing the triumph of 'I am loved!' Ah the magnificence, the triumphant magnificence of 'Us! – Just look at Us!' You seemed to beam out at the town that old victory call, 'Look at us.'

And I smiled for days just to think of it. So what can you do for me? You'll teach me courage, will you? For life? You who had none for love? Such cowardice will always mark you. How do I know these things? Me, this middle-aged Irish-Catholic woman? I could tell you that a man and a woman and a life together is a bedtime story. The rest is only lovely when that's what's keeping it all true. You see, that's what a man and woman need to know. Children whip up a storm of love all right and leave you so tired with loving them and caring for them that a whole lifetime can be eaten up by them. Yes, once you're tricked into that you've got no chance of escape. But if it's a piece of heaven for you when you roll into bed and feel the man or woman you want moving beside you, ah then the whole thing is different. I could tell you these things now, Brendan, because I've known you since you were a child and I know well your mother wouldn't give you the same story. Indeed I know she didn't. Mothers can be mean to chil dren, hiding things like the truth from them then dressing the lie up as love. The world is drowning in the lies parents tell their children. I would not have lied to him, my beautiful boy. I would have told him the truth.

Oh but Sissy you lied to yourself that day. You ran away, Sissy, because you couldn't look at what you'd half-glimpsed that day in that back garden. The wounds. Or what you heard. The noise. The calling out. Stop! Stop! I am frozen in the deepest part of hell. Are my thoughts sinful? The sin of malice? Malice. Why even the word has the hiss of the snake about it. I could become like Betty Shaughnessy. Betty Shaughnessy who lost her twin brother, ten years later still waiting for others to join her club of perpetual mourners. Happy to see others weep as she's wept. Driving her husband Ray to drink and to women. Tom will never do that. His very soul is mine. Nothing and no one on God's earth could take him from me. Who else can say this? No, I don't feel malice. But what can this young man do for me? Can he howl down the howling? No. He cannot. He got love wrong. What can he do well?

'Mrs O'Hara you've been like this for months now.'

Months! The man makes it sound like an eternity. Youth!

'And Dr Sullivan and I have talked, and you've been observed now for a week.'

That can't be true! A week? What a gamester time is. Plays months and a week to the same tune. A tune played on a concertina. A week! Can that be true? What is happening to me?

'And we are very worried. You are in such a deep place.'

First good line he's spoken.

'You know, I studied at the Maudsley and there is a technique, a treatment.'

Is there a treatment? Is it new – a new treatment for such ancient pain? I don't know. If I wait, he'll tell me.

'We've talked, Dr Sullivan and I, about Electro-Convulsive Therapy.'

Have you indeed, Brendan? I laugh inside myself. Electro-Convulsive Therapy. I'm convulsed. Well, I suppose that's what he trained for. To be able to say a line like that and not laugh! It sounds irreligious as well. I wonder if it's been sanctioned by the church. They're not keen on psychiatry. God has all the answers and he communicates them through the priest, who probably doesn't want any competition. I suppose it's a surprise we ever got this hospital.

'We don't know exactly how it works.'

That's honest of him.

'Sometimes there is a risk that short-term memory will be impaired.'

What is he talking about? Short-term memory? What a child this man is.

'In a sense, the therapy shocks you back into life.'

One shock to kill another.

'There'll be a few sessions but there's no guarantee.'

Well now, I'm not a great believer in guarantees any more Brendan.

'But I must emphasise the risk. The risk is of some memory loss. Possibly more than some. Can you understand what I'm saying to you Sissy?'

But memory is the pain. Maybe. Maybe I like the sound of that machine, of a ruthless little machine going into my head and twisting the odd screw here and there. Isn't that how they describe mental illness? She's got a screw loose. Maybe the machine will tighten it up.

'You're in a deep place of shock and grief and we've got to shock you back to us. We must get you back to us.'

To us? And who might 'us' be? The arrogance! But we're not an arrogant race. Too careful for arrogance. We think the British are arrogant. I never found them so. Always seemed a bit uneasy to me. They say the German is arrogant. Doesn't talk much. But then do we talk much to him? He walks tall; I suppose that's a sign of arrogance. And he doesn't seem to bend under the weight of his memories. Sure, every time anyone looks at the German they can feel the weight. I suppose he's got lots of memories. Terrible memories. Bombing. And, God knows, lots of other things. We didn't want to know that much about the War. Tom insists I call it that, not the Emergency, but even afterwards we kept ourselves . . . pure? Yes that's the word. We didn't stain ourselves with the knowledge of it. Ah well I don't think the German is a bad man. There are lots of Germans around now in Ireland; some of them I suppose must be bad. But all of them? I doubt it. I could be wrong, of course. But how did he kill memory, the German? And did he? Dr Carter? He was Major in the British Army, I'm told. A doctor must see terrible things in a war. Won a cross or something. Áine, his housekeeper, found it. He swore her to secrecy. But she told me. People tell me things. They trust me. They're right. I didn't tell anyone apart from Tom. But I don't trust myself any more. And never will again. A cross! We could give them away! Yes, Dr Carter and the German. They've seen some things! Why did they come to a country dripping in memory? Maybe to drown their own. Did it work?

But where could I go? Tipperary? England? New York? Oh for God's sake! No, Tom is right. Living close to what is lost. What would we be without it, memory? Well, it'll never die here. Never in this country. We feed it too well. Still that machine, what if it worked? No, it's a mad idea. But let me think. If I could choose, what would I choose to forget? The sound? Sound sudden-shaking into a moment. Which was the last moment of my old life. Not ringing out. No. Rolling over us. Rolling us up into it. I was paralysed by sound. In my own kitchen. The rim of the teacup trembling on the edge of my lips and me looking at Olivia stretching her hand out for the country butter to heap onto the brown bread I made myself, hovering between the brown bread and the soda bread, greedy and not certain which plate her hand should land on . . . And then the Sound. Would we be killed by Sound? That's what I thought: my God, we're going to be killed by Sound! No wonder I want silence. I will always want silence.

And then the look between us! Our eyes and heads were twinned things. Moving in unison to look at the swinging door through which he'd walked and then. The scream. Mine. 'He's in the yard!' He wasn't. He was in the back garden. Half in and lying half out of it, as I found out in a second, after the Sound. And after the running. The running. Did I run? Yes. Yes. The running and the second's sight of him and the voice. His voice calling to us, 'Get a doctor and a priest quickly.' And then, oh take these words away. Take them away. 'Turn me over quickly. Don't let my mother see me.' Or should I carve it on my breast? On my left breast above my heart? 'Turn me over quickly and don't let Mama see me.' Could his time machine kill that?

'It involves passing an electrical current through the brain for a short period of time. There'll be a number of sessions. We'll give you a muscle relaxant, Sissy, because the current causes convulsions. And there are physiological and biochemical changes.'

Change my mind, would you Brendan? A change of mind. A shocking change of mind. Sissy changed her mind and came back to life. A miracle.

'I know it sounds brutal, Sissy, but . . .'

Brutal? It sounds exactly what I need.

'You will be given an anaesthetic and a muscle relaxant, Sissy.'

Anaesthetised, he says, and I wonder at the word. I'm sedated enough in this place not anaesthetised so the pain of nothingness gets through. Now he's talking about pain. He's still on about pain. How it won't be there. No pain will visit me. But I want pain. Physical pain. I have a need of another kind of pain.

'It might not happen in your case. You might not suffer any memory loss at all.'

So it might all be for nothing. Oh Brendan!

'I would never be anything else but honest with you Sissy.'

Ah – he's hopeless! Never be less than honest? Poor Brendan doesn't seem to know there's no one gets through life without sometimes being a liar. Particularly to themselves. Do you think I would have lived the day out if I'd have seen my child, bits of him scooped out? I lied to myself. I would not believe. I wrapped it all up in a lie, the lie of my life and ran into the place I'm in now. Frozen here in my terrible lie. 'Come to bed. He's going to be all right. We'll go in the morning.' Oh I knew. I knew.

'I don't know, Mrs O'Hara . . .'

He's back to Mrs O'Hara. Regrets the intimacy, I suppose. Maybe it's unprofessional.

'I don't know if you understand how ill you are.'

My God this boy is brilliant! Dripping in wisdom. Dripping in it.

'What happened, Mrs O'Hara, to your family . . . well a death like that . . . an explosion, like a bomb . . .'

Was it like a bomb? Maybe. I suppose he's right. An explosion . . . a bit like a bomb. Yes. But I suppose it could have happened in the school lab. But bombs, we have no bombs here. We know nothing of bombs down here. Not in this town. Oh a few in 1940: the Germans lost their way, evidently. But they paid compensation. Which is more than the British ever paid over the centuries. And of course there was May 1941, that May bank holiday. The North Strand, Dublin, got the worst of it. How many killed? So we suffered a bit. But really, bombing was for the Six Counties. And the British. Did we feel sorry enough for them? We took it all a bit calmly. And we'd exploded a few ourselves in . . . when? Was it 1939? Before the Emergency? The War. Sorry Tom, sometimes I forget. Ha! We were sorry for Belfast. Their love of Britain came at a price. Yes we were sorry, and for England, for London especially. But it wasn't happening to us. And we'd suffered enough for centuries. Why is my mind doing this? Making such quick, mixed-up connections. Connected to electricity. That's what will happen to me. Because I'm sad in a dangerous way. Not mad. Well, I know that. Sad. Madly sad, perhaps.

'The shock of what happened, Mrs O'Hara, has made you close down the energy system. We might be able to . . .'

I'd laugh if I could remember how to make that sound. Is he going to jump-start me? Like a car? What would happen if I began to run out of control? And crashed? It's strange to be numb and in agony at the same time, and to have the little brain God gave me get suddenly quick and clever like that daughter of mine. I never could abide people who talk the way I think-talk now. When you don't care about much you can be very clever. And nothing clever is ever gentle. They're all mind, the clever ones. Never the outstretched hand, the little squeeze of the fingers to just show they cared about your trouble, large or small. I'd sit for hours in the car with Tom or go for walks with him. All we did was talk and not a clever word between us and our souls, Brendan. Not your kind of clever.

'How did you meet Tom?'

Ah, the marriage story, is that what you want Brendan? An education? A few signposts? The lovers. You want the story, Brendan? Here it is. Easier in parts to tell than it was to live. I'm a wayward woman now Brendan. Perhaps I should warn him. I could do him harm today.

'Mrs O'Hara. How did you meet Tom?'

I'm right. This is his way of getting me to feel again. Pathetic! Through memory? The memory of a feeling is as hard to catch as a butterfly, and in my opinion catching butterflies is a cruel sport. Though I'm trying to catch one that's flying around in my head. Read somewhere that you forget the sound of the voice. I don't have his voice. No little recording, you know. My cousins in America used to write to me, wanted to send me their home movies. I used to mock them. Home movies, for God's sake! What I'd give for a home movie of him now. Or a recording . . . To hear him talking and doing his 'Sarsfield is the word and Sarsfield is the man' stuff, jumping on the bed with one of my old scarves tied around his shoulders like a cloak and brandishing the wooden sword Tom made him. And what was the other line he loved? Oh yes. Robert Service, 'The Shooting of Dan McGrew' . . . '"Boys," says he, "you don't know me, and none of you care a damn."'

The child thought damn was a bad word. Ah well. Now, where is Brendan in his place of word-work? Brendan, the labourer in the field of silence trying to plough up words, trying to sow kindness and gather in a harvest of words. But the labourer looks tired. Come on now! I'm surprised at you, Brendan.

'Mrs O'Hara, I'll talk to Tom again and we'll talk again and then see how we go. I'll call Nurse Daly now and she'll take you back to your room.'

I have my own room here. Dr Sullivan has pull, as they say. Or perhaps they want to keep me away from the others in case I make them worse. Nurse Daly arrives. Lively, a cock-robin kind of girl. She smiles at me. I suppose she's sincere.

'Hello Sissy. Here, take my arm.'

Oh God! My arm! Does that woman know what she has said? No. She does not. She rattles on. Loving me with talk.

'My mother said to tell you she is praying for you at Mass every morning. She knew your mother you know, in Offaly, God rest her soul.'

Not even God himself could rest that woman's soul. My mother was on fire with the love of Ireland. Her meetings of Mná na hÉireann, Women of Ireland, as important to her as Mass and certainly more important than her daughters. Her sons fared better in the love stakes. Oh she worked hard for love. Love of country. Love of her hero brother, worship of the memory of Joe, who'd made her father the proudest man in Wexford. The debt we all owed Joe would be unpaid until what he'd died for, a united Ireland, came about. And then off she'd go. Robert Emmet's speech from the dock, lines from Wolfe Tone, dazzling my boys when she came on her annual visit. Tom trying to be kind to a woman whose head and heart were so twisted in one direction she'd never be straight. 'She's not really interested in you at all. Not in any of you,' Tom said the first time he visited her. He was right. She just assumed she knew us all. As if the fact that she had given birth to us gave her access to our souls whether we liked it or not. She was convinced she could foretell what we'd do. The strange thing was that she was right about that. Almost. When I took Tom home that day to meet her she looked at the two of us and sighed long and loud to make sure we heard it clearly. Later, when I was alone with her in the kitchen, she put her two hands flat on the table and stared at me. Drummed the fingers for a minute or so. 'You've gone for that life, have you?' 'What life?' 'Oh, that old dream,' she'd said. Before I could ask 'what dream?' she raised her hands before her face, hiding it. 'The love dream,' she'd said. 'Body and soul in a love dream.' And I'd blushed at the word body, like a child. And then I'd remembered the same savage look in her face, a kind of hunger when she looked at my father when I was small, and which I thought had meant she was cross with him. And I think now, after all these years, maybe I was wrong about that look. Maybe after he died she substituted one love dream for another. He died young, my father William. And she said nothing much. Sent us all to her sister for a week, in Limerick. We were terrified though my Aunt Breda was kind enough. When we went home the house had been spring cleaned. He'd gone. All of him gone, in the cleaning. She never spoke again about him. That hiding of her face – that gesture which I would interpret differently in years to come – that night I understood it to mean that the conversation was over. She cut me with silence that night. Usually she cut me with words. She could cut both ways all right. And that little smile she kept for her girls, her daughters, none of us as brilliant as she, nor half as good-looking. Three daughters she brought into the world in order to get one son, then she got another. Two boys after three girls. Me first, then Clara, then Stella, the three disappointments, while she held out for what she wanted: boys. None of her daughters 'were a patch on her. There was no comparison.' Which was true. She wounded each of us equally. Fair's fair. Clara, named after my mother's birthplace. What a mother! 'Clara,' she'd say, 'you're a pretty little madam, but you've got the ambition of the respectable poor. You want a quiet life and a clean house and a husband who'll go to the top of some clerical department, or middle in the civil service or maybe top man on the middle floor.' And Clara did. And seems happy enough. And

Stella! 'Ah Stella, star of no sea.' And every time my mother told her little joke Stella would smile. Tortured young and loving the torturer. Does it get any worse? My mother nearly broke Stella with her rage the day Stella cut her hair. 'A desecration' that she could not understand, winding the long black plait of her own hair round and round that neat little head of hers and in revenge rechristening Stella Steve, after her favourite jockey who, though English, had an Irish name and had won something or other. 'Steve suits her better. She's got less hair now than half the men I know. You had great hair, Stella. It was your only claim to beauty. If I were you I'd marry the first man that asks you. There won't be a queue.' And Stella, thereafter called Steve, did marry the first man who asked her. Who was handsome and tall, which my mother 'liked in a man'. 'Well, well!' she exclaimed when she first saw him. 'And where did Steve find you? Where on earth did she find you?' 'I found her,' he'd said. And Steve, who stood rosy and smiling the smile of a fulfilled and grateful woman who knew she'd brought home treasure, told me later that she'd 'nearly fainted with pleasure'. That had been a triumph all right. One of the few over a mother who'd laboured to bring into the world five children when her maternal instincts would have been easily satisfied with two, both of them boys. One of whom, Joe, named after her hero-brother, heavy burden that, looked a bit like Pearse – Patrick,

133

that is (no one seems to have an image of poor Willie Pearse, his brother, who was also executed; his face just never caught on, I suppose) – and the other, Brian, who didn't look like any kind of Irish hero, though my mother hid her disappointment. He was a boy, after all. Joe and Brian both went on to be teachers in England, where I don't suppose there's much call for the story of Patrick Pearse. I loved my brothers, but on they went into another world and since my mother died we don't hear much of them. They came home for the burial. Then it was over. We're at the end of the corridor now and Nurse Daly guides me into my room and sits me down.

'Here we are Sissy. Didn't Dr Sullivan get you a nice little room in the new wing. Would you like some tea, Sissy?'

I nod.

'I'll get it for you and sure I'll sit with you for a while. I'm about to go off duty but I'll sit with you and we'll have a little chat.'

A little chat! No we won't Nurse Daly. For you? You think I'll speak for you?

'My granny went out with Joe, your mother's brother. Did you know that, Sissy?'

I nod and remember that my mother told me that half the girls in the village later claimed they'd gone out with Joe, proud of the association with a hero.

'The man was a hero, Sissy. After he died my

granny used to visit the house. Photographs of him in the sitting room and all the way up the stairs. And a copy of the Proclamation of Independence in every room. Almost as many as the Blessed Virgin. Do you know what I think, Sissy? Maybe it runs in the family.'

What is she talking about? What does?

'Yes, heroism! Maybe it runs in the family.'

She looks at me admiringly with her small brown eyes. What's an Irish girl doing with brown eyes? Heroism? What is she saying? I keep staring at her.

'The lad, Sissy, I'm sure if he'd lived he would have been a great man for the cause. He would have been a hero. That's what a few people in the town think. Sure he had all the ingredients. Didn't he win a competition for Pearse's "Boys of Ireland" speech? Am I right about that? God Sissy, my head's a bit gone. I'm engaged to a man who thinks Daniel O'Connell was Ireland's greatest hero. All O'Connell did was talk, Sissy. It comes between us. Declan never told me in the beginning. I mightn't have let things go so far. Still, he's just been made manager of the new creamery. He'll be a good husband. I come from a staunch Republican family. I tell you, Sissy, peaceful negotiation never worked with Albion! We'll never get the North back through peaceful negotiation. Anyway, Sissy, we need the boys of Ireland to believe in heroes and Brother Rory – he's a cousin, you know – says the lad was a real genius at science . . . chemicals – all that kind of stuff . . .'

. . . and I feel the sound coming and it's rolling over me, it's rolling, rolling over me . . . and I stand up suddenly and I throw my head back and I scream.

CHAPTER 9

They tell me I've been asleep for a day and a bit. Tom's just left, coming back in an hour. Olivia is still here, sitting on a chair by my bed, staring at me. She's defiant. She is going to outface this shame. She won't give me any quarter. A warrior girl. How did Tom and I breed a warrior girl? She's a young angel of vengeance, knowing she's been the one tested in the fire and hadn't failed. She's looking at her supposed protector, her mother, with such contempt. Ah, the contempt of the young! The anger! My daughter is very angry. She's very young and she's very brave. I am a coward. She looks at me and still sees a mother, and I look at her and I don't see my child any more. I see this girl, separated from me. And lost and sad and terribly angry. Like she's banging on a window begging me to open it so that she can fly in again but it's locked. She believes I have the key. That I simply will not give it to her. Perhaps she thinks I threw it away in order to keep her out. Maybe she's right.

'When will you come home?'

I must find words. With her I have no choice.
She will not let me hide. She will not allow me
silence. I look around the room. Go on, Sissy, I
say to myself. The words are flying around here.
Catch them. Go on, just a few. Let them sound.
I owe her words.

I must try.

'Soon, Olivia, soon.'

There, I've spoken. Words. I've prised open the
world of talk. What a place it is. And the minute
you start more talk is demanded. You make a few
sounds. Then someone sounds back at you. Good
manners, they say.

'When?'

Oh God. Where did you come from, Olivia?
My darling Olivia?

'When I'm better.'

Can't do better than that. It's all that comes out.
Sounds bad? Bad sound?

'You look OK to me.'

She's your daughter. Try to talk to her. Slowly.
If I speak slowly each word will matter. She will
know I'm trying. Why not try a long sentence?

'I'm not OK. I need this time here with the
doctors.'

'When will you come home?'

'Olivia, if I don't stay here I will never get better.'

'What's wrong with you? I don't know what's
wrong with you.'

What's wrong with me Olivia? You know what's
wrong with me. Oh I think you do. But I can't

say that to her. Though it's a good long sentence, that. Yes, that's a longer sentence.

'I'm very sick, Olivia.'

'We're all very sick. But you're the only one in hospital.'

She knows it's a mean few words she's spoken. She's a word-terrorist. Who will she destroy with words? She goes on.

'I can't cook.'

Sure she's a child still! Oh darling. The sound of those words could almost break the ice of the frozen lake I'm in. Almost. Now Sissy, try to be a mother to her. Talk to her more.

'I know you can't cook, darling, but mucking along for a while won't kill you. And you've got Sally. She comes in every day. She helps. Tell me how you manage.'

Does this sound kind?

'I don't like Sally in the house. I feel invaded.'

Oh, has she upset Sally? Who helps, but is a bit tricky. Does it matter? Listen, she's still talking.

'I do breakfast in the morning, cereal and things, and then we do soup and stuff in the evening. Dada does the meat.'

'Sounds good.'

'Daragh misses your apple tarts.'

You could almost make me cry. You're getting close, Olivia.

'I tried to teach you.'

'I never wanted to learn.'

That's true enough. You'd set about that pastry

with such contempt that you pounded it into submission. You've got too heavy a hand for pastry making. 'It's the ugliest looking thing anyway,' you said. Hated the colour of it. Hated it. And no matter how often Tom said to you, 'You don't *hate* the colour of pastry, Olivia, you *dislike*,' it never worked. No half measures with Olivia. She doesn't understand the concept. Which is why she can't make my famous apple tart. Though she devours it. Well it's a nothing thing, I suppose. But everyone loved them. Every time anyone in the street – and indeed not only in this street – was expecting a visitor they'd ask me, 'Sissy, would you make one of your apple tarts for me? Everyone loves them.' Though once when I boasted, what a foolish thing but human I suppose, Olivia said, 'No. Everyone loves you. They all love you.' And she kissed me. And it's true. I am a much-loved woman. And then she said, 'Except Granny, of course.' And I remember what my mother said of Olivia: 'She's too tart for tarts.' But Olivia was right that day. Everyone didn't love me. My mother didn't really love me, or Clara or Stella. She couldn't help it. Though she loved her husband probably more than I knew, maybe even as much as Joe and Brian. Marriage is destiny, she used to say. She gave up a lot for my father. She was the best side-saddle rider in the county. Spoke French and German. Lived in a house with parkland all around it. Gave up a certain way of life to 'marry down', as they say. Yes, marriage is destiny.

Who else said that? Marjorie Brannigan! That night when Jim Brannigan was in another one of his states, and this the worst state, when he'd dangled his boys out of the window and Tom had been a hero, again, talking Jim out of it, cajoling, then threatening to 'break every bone in his bank teller's fingers' if Jim Brannigan did a thing to hurt them. And Jim was frightened of Tom and hauled his sons in and handed them over to him. Oh that awful, awful night when Marjorie sat there in our kitchen after we'd put her boys to bed with ours and told us, and herself I suppose, how she came to be sitting with neighbours, surrounded by the ruins of her life. Marjorie, who'd been the belle of the ball when she'd met her dangerous husband. When she'd been the most glamorous girl in Cork, which was not hard to believe. 'She reigned supreme,' her father had told us once, on a visit. And Tom and I were sure that it was true. We could see still the glory that was Marjorie, so tall with such long, slender legs and all that tumbling hair. And Tom and I used to smile at the way she'd swish it around as though it were a veil. 'She'd been the star of the convent as well.' Poor Marjorie, she'd probably seen her future stretch before her as an unbroken line of adoration, parents, nuns, schoolfriends, boyfriends, husband, children. And she was right about the children. But she was wrong about her husband. Wrong, because as she explained to us that night, when she was young she'd thought Jim's coldness

141

had been exciting. His way of wanting to control everything was manly. 'Sure, what did I know? I thought being a woman was flirting and playing a few innocent games with men. And the men adored me.' And we were certain they had. 'Don't you think someone should tell us before they let us loose on life?' Yes. But some things you only learn by living them. Olivia thinks she'll learn it all from books. She thinks it's the easy way to learn life. Books. She was going to 'learn everything from books'. 'You do that darling.' What else could I say? Shall I try again to talk to her? That's love. Trying again, I suppose. Oh I'm so tired. Do I have to talk? Yes.

'What are you reading now?'

'Everything!'

Everything! That's Olivia. Everything. Like what, I wonder. I don't have to ask. She's off. She's always loved writers, even more than the books I think. They're like personal friends to her. When she finds a book she likes she has to read everything ever written by the author. Then she's in love: 'I'm in love with Balzac, or Henry James . . .' Though he had the disadvantage that I introduced him to her. She likes to discover her own passions.

'Victor Hugo, Balzac, still mad about him. Ionesco, he writes mad plays. I understand them. Now.'

Oh God.

'Ibsen, Strindberg. Everything.'

'Good,' I whisper. But a whisper is better than silence. I suppose.

'Good? It's better than good. I know everything. I know the whole world through reading and I know everything about a small town: I know about convents, I know about doctors, death, mothers.'

What can I say to her? I shake my head. And I look away from her.

'I know that mothers need protection.'

Poor Olivia. I'm so sorry. I've let you down terribly. Maybe eventually, Olivia, all mothers let their children down. Or maybe mothers get careless. Will I remember this? Will this be taken from me? 'Short-term memory,' he said. To me, who never did a thing with only the short-term in mind? Will this defeat be taken from me? This defeat, by this child who when she was born was the triumph of my life? This child who first allowed me to say 'I am a mother'. Who allowed me to understand the special meaning of 'Mary, the Mother of God', that first of all she was a mother. Was this what my mother's hands to her face meant when I told her that I would marry Tom? But what else had she hoped for than that I would marry the love of my life and have children? Have I forgotten? Did I not wish to remember? Because it didn't suit me? Ah my darling Olivia, what will you remember of this terrible time? Through times to come. Decades to come? The seventies? I suppose they'll come and they'll go. And then there'll be the eighties? The nineties? 2000? What a thought! Oh I'll be gone by then. Well gone. If I get through this time I'll be gone in time to

143

come. And then? What then? After I'm gone? Long after I am gone, who will I be to you, Olivia? When I drift up and down the colonnades of your mind? This woman, this mother, as she is now? This now-mother? Will she cancel everything that was the beauty of me and you? Who will I be? Drifting in and out of your life and dreams, child? Trailing what, child? Trailing what? Trailing love, child? My love, child . . . Oh trailing love . . . Or trailing what?

CHAPTER 10

. . . and from the day my mother walked back into our house she seemed to be her old self again. The old self we'd all loved. She'd slipped behind the event and gone back to who she was before. Or so it seemed to us. Perhaps a brain scan could follow the trail, trace the indentation or the scars as the tissue of memory had been burned out of her. I've learned a few things about ECT since then. The majority of patients evidently respond well. Now that's a shock, to play with the word. Yes, perhaps neuroscience could ascertain the truth. But she is dead now. So I will never know. Besides, why should I prove one way or another who or what worked the miracle? She came back to herself. To her old self. That's all. That's everything.

And she said little that first day she returned to us. To me, shamefully full of shame still, to my father, full of longing, a man waiting to be plugged back into life, and to Daragh, who seemed to have painted blank-white over everything and who smiled straight at us, when what we wanted was just the hint of a shadow playing within the brilliant light of that famous Daragh smile. Some hint of a shadow, which would assure us that he understood.

She wore pale blue the day she came back. The black was gone. She'd put it away or left it behind her I suppose, with the rest of what she'd left behind her, like slipping out of a habit, black serge on the floor. Yes. She was into the blue again. He'd bought her a new pale blue twinset. 'I'll help you Dada,' I'd said when he'd set out for Miss Coyle's drapery shop with a determined look on his face. 'No. No, child. I'd like her to know her normally colour-blind husband did it himself. Besides, if I'm confused as to the shade I'll remember her eyes. I was never colour-blind to those eyes. Was I ever blind to those eyes?' 'No, Dada,' I'd nodded. And that day, the day she came back, the expression in those high-blue eyes of hers seemed to me to be the same as of old. Honestly! Though I suppose were I to lie, how would you know?

We were aware that day, the day she came back, that she would have to walk around the house. Sooner or later. And better to start right away, on that first day. The house needed to be possessed again. Perhaps it needed to know we could, and would, go on. It wasn't a large house, the walk-about would not take long. Still, we all knew it was a momentous journey and fraught with many perils. And when she arrived at his room! Our hearts! The beat of them! And we waited, afraid to move or to say anything. I watched her hands.

146

Was there a tremor of hesitation before she opened the door? Then her face. I looked at her face, which demanded from me more courage than I'd imagined.

I was willing her to soldier on. And she did. She was leading us, I suppose. Her gaze, it seemed to me, was steady. But she did not test her strength too hard, which was a kindness to us. She bowed her head for a second and moved on to my room, which was all neat and tidy. I'd made preparations for a visitor. That's a way of looking at it. Who knows? Who knows anything? After her tour she sat down in her chair in the kitchen. And there was the hint of a smile. Honestly.

'My God Tom! The house looks spotless. Are you trying to put me out of a job?'

The relief! They say it floods over you, and as a description there's not much wrong with it. But it doesn't quite get that stomach thing, the way relief makes the muscles untwist and you start to breathe calmly.

'Well we worked all night. Didn't we, children?'

And we, the chorus, smaller now, answered together.

'Yes we did, Dada.'

And she, in that awful gentleness of hers, smiled again. Yes. It was quite clearly a smile.

'And you on your Easter holidays. Thank you, Daragh. Thank you, Olivia.'

And we told her she looked grand.

'You look grand. Really grand, Mama.'

147

'Well you haven't seen me for a while; not really, not the old me.'

Yes. She actually said that. The phrase rings clearer now that I haven't seen her in years and would give . . . What? Almost anything to see her again. Well, up to the point of sacrificing those I love now who are alive, here, with me. Selfish, you see, still, to the last. Anyway, back to that day . . .

'I went on a journey,' she said, 'and they thought it best if I went alone. Though I was grateful for your visit, after the incident in the hospital. You remember, Olivia?'

'Yes, Mama. I remember.'

'I hope, in time, you'll forget,' she said.

But I never have.

'I thought you were in the hospital all the time. So where else did you go, Mama?' asked Daragh, with that weird innocence of his. It was as good a shield as anything else, his innocence. It went straight to the point and then straight past it. It's the way he got through, I suppose.

'Ah nowhere you'd want to follow me,' and she bowed her head at that.

'Do you know, Dada?' asked Daragh.

And on he went, Daragh, with a look on his face that implied he was trying to help the conversation by giving it a little push. And my father, knowing everything, knew when to exclude him.

'I do Daragh. But that's between us.'

And she did her bit. She knew the moment was

dangerous and that something, a few words at least, were required of her.

'Daragh, you can go back to playing your music. Now that I'm home.'

Oh his face! The light!

'Are you sure, Mama?'

And my father, in the glow of Daragh's smile, said, 'He can beam, that boy, can't he Sissy?'

And they were right. He could beam in and out of smiles, and down airwaves – after he left. And he rang us often, after he left. In the beginning.

'Are you sure Mama?' he asked again.

'Of course I am, Daragh.'

'Ah that's great. That's great.'

'Let me make you some tea Mama.'

'Thank you, darling.'

'Look Sissy! It's snowing. Come to the window.'

And at that we trembled. The window! And all it looked out on. And all it looked back on. Maybe, through snow? Softer? Maybe through snow.

'Let me see! Ah! Ah Tom! The snow! And oh . . . oh . . .'

And oh God how I shook inside. Please hold on, I begged her silently, please hold on.

And she did.

'And Tom, you got the gate! You never told me,' she said.

As though we were talking about just a gate! And I thought, she's done it! She's through!

'I wanted to surprise you Sissy. Something new

for you, for your coming-home day. Not that it's new, of course.'

'No. Who'd make a gate like that now? So the German gave it to you after all?'

'He did. And sent Tim down to help. And Bogus came over and even Jim Brannigan helped, and Father Dwyer said he'd bless it for us whenever we want.'

'It looks great. It makes the place, that place, well . . . it's such an important gate. You'd think you were going into a huge garden, all laid out. And for him. It's . . . ah now, now . . . I'll have that tea now Olivia. Sorry. I'm doing all right now. Don't worry, just a little moment. Memory, you know. Just for a minute. Gone now. All gone now.'

CHAPTER 11

I remember that 'all gone now'. And it seemed to be true. Her old self seemed to be back with us, and since the old self had been so very loved by us we wanted it back. Very much. It was what we'd prayed for, even me, and done novenas for, had gone to Mass for. And our prayers were answered and peace came back into our house. And she walked anywhere and everywhere, into all the rooms, including his, and they went for their walks, the Start-rite kids, holding hands, talking, always talking. Though of one thing they never talked, at least not to Daragh and me. Over time our questions grew as the more we learned about her treatment, little snippets here and there, the more we wondered, had it worked? Or was she just being good to us? As she'd always been, good to us. But apart from that story they seemed to talk of everything and seemed to understand everything and to accept everything and to absolve everyone, delighting even in their little foibles: in Bogus Brogan, in what she called the sweetness of his vanity; in May Garvey, whose previous harsh brilliance with words had made each one sound angular somehow and who now fashioned her conversation into a single poem, a lyric of triumphant motherhood, unable to rustle up any of her old witticisms and criticisms of our national obsession with history or of Yeats's dream-world, now that she was in her own and had mastered its new language, in which every sentence would contain the words 'my son', in a voice that my mother said would almost 'sparkle out of her' when she spoke of 'my son, Phil,' named after her husband because 'you can never have too many Phil Garveys in the world'. May told my mother she'd once thought of naming him 'after the lad' but thought it best not to. And my mother agreed. I too thought it a wise decision. When they talked of the Brannigans and of what it was had happened to Jim Brannigan, they looked for ways to understand. They were certain it had happened young to him, happened early and that it had grown something in him, something gnarled that had made him so fierce with fear and hatred of his boys that he'd dangled them out the window to terrify them. Someone hadn't loved him enough and, maybe more than that, some weakness in him, some blindness, had made him not see where love lay. For it lay close to him, in his own adult home with Marjorie the magnificent, with her tumbling brown-haired beauty and her long, long legs, 'an occasion of sinful thoughts to many' as Bogus used to say, with a wink even a nun would not object to. And they talked of Eamonn and the love of his life, which was mechanical, for he worshipped the cold and gleaming perfection of the bishop's Mercedes. They laughed at Eamonn's foot-on-the-accelerator driving: 'the closest he would ever come to power in his life,' my father said. They noted the bishop's great affection for Eamonn and they spoke in awe of the bishop's daily demonstration, as he sat serenely in the back of the car, of his absolute faith in the goodness of God. And Daragh and I would hug these bits of wisdom, half-overheard, during the four years we stayed, after the event, to be with them, to listen to them and to witness the miracle. And though we would forget many seemingly important things that were taught us in the long school of life we didn't forget those lessons in the years that were waiting for us. Which were – and this is natural – more numerous than theirs.

CHAPTER 12

And in those years I left Ireland. It was late in a decade that was beating a wild-rhythm celebration by boy-men called Mick and Paul and John who were rolling all over us. Though not over me. Nor over many who remained in the place I'd left, who certainly heard the music but missed the message. And would get it later, much later. When boys called Bob and Bono would bring their own wild-rhythm celebration and the world would fall down in worshipful hallelujahs as it again acknowledged Ireland's capacity to create missionaries. So what if they were 'the boys in the band'? They sang from a pulpit, an enormous pulpit looking down on a congregation that would knock your eyes out. A city that had produced Joyce and Beckett and Yeats, a country that produced poet-heroes and more priests and nuns per head of population than almost any on earth was not going to spawn boys who just wanted to stand before a packed hall of gyrating teenagers and strum their guitars and sing. They had to have a message. One of salvation; they were in it to save the world. Like I said, we're teachers, missionaries.

I left when I thought my time at home with my parents was finished. When I was certain that they no longer needed me. And I bumped into a life. Many people do. I worked in theatre. That phrase alone tells you I had no vocation for it. I stumbled into acting. It happens. Rarely. It suited me. The disciplined dreaming, the timed surrender to the putting-away of self. At which I became adept. A double life, one that required a daily performance, the same part. They 'got me', as they say. I was Irish, very Irish. 'Enough said,' as we say – in Ireland. I believe I gave a performance that was true to life and its expected truth, which they believed they discerned just in the sound of my voice. People hate surprises, particularly sound surprises. And the living life of the imagined world, my remembered world and its people and their voices, that went on of course, through the hours of the days of performance as they beat their way steadily down to 'Five minutes to curtain, Miss O'Hara.' Miss O'Hara, who made a bit of a name; reliable third lead, I suppose you could call it. 'She brings her usual precise intelligence to the small but nevertheless important part of . . .' I had one or two triumphs. Everyone does. Everyone gets something to hold on to. *Ivanov* was mine, the part of Anna, the dying wife, watching her husband's future with Sasha unfold before her fading eyes. What an image to take to the grave. Ivanov followed her quickly enough – though not for love. Savage play for a twenty-seven-year-old to write. But then some lessons are learned early.

I was better than good as Anna but that's all. Which is not enough for many, but it was for me. I was offered a season at the National and a film. To which I said no, to my own amazement, never mind anyone else's. I'd decided I was happy where I was. Third lead, some decent TV, the classics, Dickens, always reliable, radio, talking books, some teaching, then more teaching. All the while I was looking for something. I found it. But that's another story. The film role made the name of the girl who played it, 'big time', as they say. As though time could ever be increased or cut down to size. But I'm a careful person when on life's surface, the surface that for many gives some recognisable shape to the experience. Only a fool plays with fame, as fame is played now, a lethal game of mathematics in which body and soul are weighted with the essential audience that hangs like an albatross around both. The goal, when you score it, ensures that you will be known by more people than you know, since the people you know are clearly not satisfying enough. Fame is toxic to those who dare not test the thinness of the ice. The weight could bring them down. Warriors, in the ancient world, put their souls away for safe keeping during times of danger. I'd put mine away and didn't want strangers to search for it. I might lose it. I'd watched those who'd thrown their souls in front of strangers and their bemusement when it was handed back to them, marked and scratched. Sometimes they didn't even get it back. Well, they'd been careless. Some of them wept, of course. But it was too late. It's murderously difficult to get your soul back, in any condition, once you've let it slip away from you. There's no search party willing going out in all weathers to find your lost soul. So I was careful, or maybe I just lacked the courage.

Over the years I laid a structure on what I believed were shaky foundations, and lived long enough to reverse that assessment. But, like I said, that's another story. If you've got time. Someday, not today. But the note in my voice will be different when I tell it. *In voce veritas*. It's a lovely story, a kind of miracle. But it's not for now. On this story, the one I'm telling you, shadows fall on the landscape of my heart and they have no fault lines. Shadows never do and as they slip away, as shadows do, a mist descends so thick it almost chokes me, like drifting smoke from embers, and I find it hard to breathe so the rhythms of my voice become different. Slower. Heavier. The words are weighted. They could carry me down. Down through dark waters. But I resist their current. I'm a long-distance swimmer. We keep on to the shore. Our stroke beats constant on the water. One-two-three, one-two-three, one-two-three. Yes. I am built for the long haul, for seeing things through to the end. So I swim on, often exhausted, above the deep dark, through the rivers of unending silence broken only by the steady breathing in and out of my incantation, one-two-three, one-two-three, one-two-three. I owe them that. I owe my parents that at least. The memory of their battle was an order from on high. Do not fail us. Do not fail life. These orders, which in time resonated from their graves, are, I believe now, the very soul of action. Sometimes, of course, out of reverence for the dead, we ignore the fact that the voices of the dead do not always command us to life and its living, as theirs had. No, sometimes the dead whisper-shout other commands.

CHAPTER 13

Of the event on that searing summer day in Ireland and, in time, indeed of him I rarely spoke. I learned that reticence is a benediction, a kind of grace. For on those rare occasions when I did break my silence – and love always had something to do with it – I found that after the story there was no way back. The listeners, the few that heard, heard only words and the words made them uneasy. I had burdened them. And, as I discovered, love, sexual love, is not designed to carry such a burden. That particular love is naturally selfish. Looking back I remember that sometimes I just stumbled to the edge, almost, of the conversation, a little too much wine perhaps, or tiredness, maybe a weariness, or some echo in a line, 'glass splinters are stuck in my tongue'. I never said anything very specific, just once or twice . . . you know the kind of thing, a response to the search by others for signals that might lead to intimacy. 'Do you come from a large Irish family?' 'No,' I'd say, and leave it at that. If someone got very close I might say, 'I had a brother who died.' Best not to go further. If I mention my sister it all becomes mathematical, a kind of numbers game.

Anyway, once I went further – just blurted out – 'Sometimes when I hear the sound of an ambulance, I freeze . . . then I shake . . . then it passes . . . though I feel weak . . . sometimes for hours.' And I told him everything. Almost. Maybe it was the strangled intensity with which I choked the words out that was so shocking, or the passionate grief all caught up in my tearless, blazing eyes that implied such a love for another, which led to the idea that 'something must be done'. Men in love wish for no competition from anyone, dead or alive. Possession is at stake. Possession is an absolute when one is absolutely in love. And he was. 'I am absolutely in love . . . it's overwhelming.' And I used to think, well, that's what it's meant to be. It's meant to overwhelm you. Still, I was sympathetic. It's terrifying, the 'absolutely in love' time. 'It breaks my heart to see you suffer . . . Don't you think you should talk to someone?' 'I'm talking to you.' 'I know, but it's clearly so painful. You don't seem to have come to terms with it.' A term that has always struck a peculiarly legalistic note, as though one could bargain with the dead, or their representatives on earth, who are not always fully briefed. 'I want to help you. I am so desperately in love with you. And when I see you in this pain it's awful. I feel rejected, I suppose. I feel you keep me . . . outside.' And that, of course, is the heart of the matter.

160

My heart, my soul were indeed occasionally elsewhere. In a place in which I could not be reached.
A door had been closed against love. Is it any
wonder that a lover would strive to break it down?
So I surrendered – for love, though not for the
love of my life, which was sad for the other,
because for the love of my life I could, and would,
and did, do anything. Do everything. Absolutely
in love is indeed absolutely overwhelming. But for
this love, which was overwhelming for him though
not for me, an injustice of the heart, I went to see
a psychiatrist. 'Jack Harrington. Young. Very
young. You'll like that.' And I thought, you're
wrong. But he continued, 'He's just starting out.
My cousin had an affair with his sister, beautiful
girl. Will you do it for my sake?' It was a small
thing to ask. I said yes. 'For your sake.' And he
smiled with such radiance I thought, go on
Olivia . . . it's a nothing thing he's asked you.

'Miss O'Hara?' He came himself into the waiting
room. Which surprised me. It was Harley Street,
after all: I expected a secretary to come for me.
But then he was only starting out, though clearly
from a privileged base. I stood up. I was older and
taller than he was. Not a good beginning. I
followed him, and I know it's a cliché but it was
up a winding staircase that I followed him into a
very sparsely furnished room. He motioned me
to sit down and carefully positioned himself in his
own chair, which itself seemed positioned at a
precise angle. Perhaps one that he'd discovered

allowed him a clearer view of the soul. I came straight to the point. Which saved us both valuable time. 'I don't really want to be here. I'm doing this for love,' I said. He was silent for a moment. Then, 'That's a good enough reason.' I assessed him. A patient has some privileges. His hair was very dark, pale skin, Irish colouring though everything else about him was English. Conventionally dressed. Manicured nails. Something slightly cruel about him. His was not a shoulder to cry on. Probably essential for him to impart that knowledge. Quickly. I started: 'It was a very hot day, in Ireland. We don't get many days when it's eighty-eight degrees.' I expected him to say, at least, 'Go on.' There was nothing. Oh God, I thought, Beckett, are we? And then, why not just go on? Let's see what he does with it? And after this I'll tell no one.

'I wore a yellow dress with daisies all along the hem. I'd been swimming in a lake, in the lake. I swim well and I walked home. It was a long walk. My mother was waiting for me. I love my mother, I thought as I sat opposite her and then I thought, I am happy. I am very happy. I'd been reading *The Portrait of a Lady*, which she'd given me. I'd read it, lying that sky-blue day on the grass verge by the lake. I read it with laughter all around me, a spinning of laughter like a mad circling of birds. For all of us were wild with astonishment that we could lie there in our swimsuits and not shiver with the cold or huddle under our towels.

162

I remember the way we called out to each other, at the wonder of it – "Isn't it s-c-o-r-c-h-i-n-g!" So, when I got home and sat there with her I told her that I'd noticed no one in the book seemed to have a proper mother. "At least, not like you," and she smiled her love back at me. "I'm near the end. Don't tell me! Will Isabel make the right decision?" "You must wait and judge, Olivia." "But what do you think, Mama?" "You must finish the book, Olivia, we'll talk . . ." and then in he came, my brother, and he said, "Hi Sis, hi Ma," and my mother and I smiled at each other. He was always getting these sayings from cowboy films, and he must have noticed because as he went out and the door slammed behind him he called out "Sorry . . . Mama" . . . and then, later, sound . . . sound was . . . Sound was a like a force, a power, like nothing I'd ever known before. It was sound, I think, that threw my mother almost to the ground . . . As she fell forward she was clutching her heart . . . is she having a heart attack? What should I do if it's a heart attack? Will my life-saving certificate help me? Maybe she's hurt her chest on the table . . . at the same time the sound: it hit the wall and the house . . . "It's coming from the back!" . . . then there was nothing . . . then "My God! He's in the back! . . . It's him! . . . He's calling! . . .'"

Then suddenly in that room in Harley Street I needed silence, again. 'Yes Miss O'Hara?'

'I want to stop. I want to stop now. I will go no

163

further. I have decided I don't want to do this. Not even for love. It seems I don't love this very nice man enough. The thing is – I just want to say this. I need to say this. I don't want to get over it. Do you understand?'

'The question, Miss O'Hara, is, do *you* understand?'

'Yes. I believe I do. I've given it a lot of thought. Leaving the past behind makes for a very short and lonely road. Anyway, I want to know what's wrong with loving someone for life? Even when they are dead?' And the words tumbled out of me, fierce, useless. 'What exactly is wrong with that? Why should I put him away, out of my mind? Like he's out of fashion. Does no one love for ever any more? Is no one built for the long road? So I carry him round. I know what it's called, "ingestion", isn't that right?' He looked at me and I knew I'd broken bounds. He was the professional here. I'd been impertinent. Or was there something else? Something I couldn't quite read. He looked away from me suddenly. And suddenly I thought, I know that look. He was remembering, someone, something. It was only a second. Then he looked back at me. Perhaps he felt it was unprofessional, after all this was my time to remember. 'Miss O'Hara—' But I cut across him. I was going to have my say and get out of there. I was not going to be robbed. 'I love him and I remember him and that's that. I only have the memory of him. Beloved. What's wrong with that? It doesn't stop me loving others. My God, isn't that what everyone wants? To be remembered by those who love them, or is it all just lies? Should people just say, "I'll love you for as long as you live, then I'm moving on"? Well I'm not leaving him behind. He's lost enough without that. I don't need to sacrifice him, again . . . and when I die, well, someone will remember me, maybe for a while . . . but not me, remembering him . . . Thank you Dr Harrington, I am leaving now.'

'Very well, Miss O'Hara. You have my number, should you change your mind.'

'Have I made the right decision?'

'Only you can answer that, Miss O'Hara.'

I saw him once again, years later at a cocktail party, though I'd heard him spoken of occasionally. It's a small town really, London. He'd built a reputation. Actually he'd built two. Brilliant and a bastard. With women. Perhaps he couldn't forget someone. Certainly the clingy creature – Cora, I heard him call her – she wasn't the one. You can tell in an instant. I didn't acknowledge him. Though I noted him. But that's what cocktail parties are for.

CHAPTER 14

And so years went by for me and for my mother and for my father. Years, for me, of parts and parties, public and private, years of phone calls from them and letters and love floating back and forth between and down the lines, and visits of course, and all that strange surprise that adult life is when one is grown up, as they say, and way beyond grown up, talking to and looking at the man and woman who made you and wondering, what was the secret of your conception? Yes, all that went on, essential news reports from my old territory that I could map for you, blindfolded, tapping out the streets by the names of those who lived in them and tapping out the road out to where I buried them.

'Now don't be angry with me, Olivia,' she said suddenly one day, during a phone call in which the living ghosts had had their story updated. And I thought, angry with you? Ah, never. At least never again.

'I've asked your father to take the gate back to the German.'

'No! I loved that gate!'

Was I angry? I don't think so. I was upset. It had looked magnificent, inappropriately magnificent. I realised I was proud of it. Proud to own it. Proud that it marked the entrance to the place where I'd heard a boy cry out 'Turn me over and don't let my mother see me', and had learned that in all my life I would never again see or hear such sweet courage. I started to cry.

'Ah Olivia. Don't, darling!'

'But what's in its place?' I asked.

'It was a magnificent gate, I know. But it's not for us, not really.'

Then I felt ashamed. Perhaps Mr Middlehoff would think us ungratefully or, worse, ill-mannered.

'What's in its place?' I asked again. 'I'm a persistent girl. She knew that.

'Nothing, nothing,' she said with a sigh. 'I've decided to leave it open. Just up the steps and you're there. No barriers. And that gate, he would have grown out of his love for it.'

What could I say to that? Mothers are always right. It was a sudden decision. But then, sometimes, she was a sudden woman. My father told me that Mr Middlehoff took the gate back with some reluctance. 'Considerable reluctance,' as he put it. He was certain that Mr Middlehoff believed it had something to do with the book he'd just published. Which was not exactly beloved by all. It dealt with his father's time in Dublin and Clonmel in the late thirties. 'This is not a story we will listen to here, Olivia. We have our own version of events. We have too good a story of our own to tell. In our own language. We don't want misinterpretations or alterations. Besides, the telling takes time. But the book had nothing at all to do with your mother's decision. She just felt the time was right. Anyway, I'm certain Mr Middlehoff believes otherwise. I think he feels insulted, and I felt a bit humiliated when I was telling him, Olivia, but your mother was insistent.' And I thought, God how he loves her! And then, it's awful how much he loves her, and then, thank God he loves her so.

CHAPTER 15

My father sent me a copy of the book. *The Visitors*, subtitle, 'Two Germans in Ireland'. The jacket mentioned his doctorate, very impressive. Flattering quotations from reviews by academic journals of his two earlier books, translated, both about Gottfried Benn, a poet I'd never heard of. What's in a name? Well, quite a lot if your name is Middlehoff and you write a book about Ireland. One that doesn't celebrate the lakes of Killarney, the lonely lunar landscape of Connemara, dear old dirty Dublin, or at least our natural charm. There was a slightly blurred photograph of Thomas Frederick – that was his second name. It didn't show how handsome he was, nor did it hint at his height – tall – which was a pity. We like tall men in Ireland.

I read the book. My father was right: Thomas Middlehoff wasn't exactly telling us what we wanted to hear. We certainly didn't want to be told by a German of his father's manoeuvres in Ireland, of his liaisons with the IRA, nor to have a detailed analysis of the Abwehr and Auslands

169

organisation which, among other aims, tried to appropriate the IRA's hatred of England for their own purposes and failed. Not a surprise. Appropriation of hatred, like the appropriation of love, is more difficult than you might think. Like stealing mercury. According to his father Erik, the IRA 'were too focused on their own aims' and were not all that interested in helping Hitler, who hadn't really featured in their plans, which were focused on England, the old defiler. My enemy's enemy was a friend all right, and friendship demands a little bit of give and take. It had been cemented over the years and here he listed key people in the cultural life of the time – a director of a national museum, a professor of sculpture, one of music – who were known Nazis. Some of whom, it seemed, like us, loved to sing out their patriotic songs and, so the story goes, at one Christmas party in 1937, 'Deutschland über Alles' and 'Horst-Wessel-Lied' and 'The Soldier's Song' resounded through a Dublin hotel, a philosophical cacophony that I found absolutely hilarious rather than sinister. Maybe it was flattering to a small contingent in our small country that, for a time, Hitler considered us vital to his success. Ireland was perhaps part of a Gaelic–Germanic domino principle. Well, as Thomas Middlehoff made clear, the plan was defeated by de Valéra, whom he described as 'Ireland's Machiavelli' – not a bad description – though of course the Prince, Michael Collins, was dead, shot in an ambush in a place called Béal na mBláth, the Mouth of Flowers. Beautiful spot, they say, though I've never been there. Thomas Middlehoff made clear that de Valéra not only kept us out of the war, he out-manoeuvred the German contingent in Ireland. But then he out-manoeuvred everyone. The Garda played their part as well. They turned out to be much more effective than any of us might have thought. Yes, the Garda, slow-looking men patrolling slowly on their bicycles, and Irish counter-espionage organisations (we were very good at it, he said) and military intelligence quietly defeated the entire enterprise. Neutral is one thing, but that's as far as it went. We weren't 'neutral on the side of Germany' as someone put it later. However I was surprised, very surprised, to learn we'd been bombed by the Germans. Quite a few times, actually, and quite a few killed – in County Wexford, County Monagahan, in County Meath, County Carlow and in County Dublin, where thirty-four were killed in 1941. You could say they bombed far and wide over a short period of time and in a small country. Was it a mistake? Were we being warned to stay neutral? Or did the British interfere with radio communications? Why hadn't anyone mentioned that part of our history at school? Why the silence? Had they forgotten? Or forgiven? Or was ancient history best packing for us?

Thomas Middlehoff offered no guidance on this one. Though he guided us to, or at least implied that, decades earlier, a shadow-doubt of pro-German sentiment had fallen on the shining beauty of 1916. Even his profound admiration for Pearse, 'one of the great orator-teachers' didn't soothe me after that defilement of our sacred text, the story of the Easter Rising. Nor did the fact that he made clear that he believed Yeats's assessment of Pearse, that he was 'mad with the desire to be Robert Emmet', to be quite simply 'incorrect'. And though he declared Pearse's 'Boy's of Ireland' speech, from which he quoted liberally, to be a masterpiece he still struck the wrong note. It was our master-piece and it seemed inappropriate of him to appropriate it. We'd been usurped before. I knew much of it by heart, the only way. Still, I tried to read it through, with a kind of distanced concentration that I thought would silence the echo and the image of a boy jumping up and down on his bed with his wooden sword in his hand. But certain lines defeated me and I was lost again.

We of Na Fianna Éireann, at the beginning of this year 1914, a year which is likely to be momentous in the history of our country, address ourselves to the boys of Ireland and invite them to band themselves with us in knightly service. We believe that the highest thing anyone can do is to serve well and truly, and we purpose to serve

Ireland with all our fealty and with all our strength.

. . . We believe, as every Irish boy whose heart has not been corrupted by foreign influence must believe, that our country ought to be free. We do not see why Ireland should allow England to govern her, either through Englishmen, as at present, or through Irishmen under an appearance of self-government. We believe that England has no business in this country at all – that Ireland, from the centre to the zenith, belongs to the Irish. Our fore-fathers believed this and fought for it: Hugh O'Donnell and Hugh O'Neill and Rory O'Moore and Owen Roe O'Neill: Tone and Emmet and Davis and Mitchel. What was true in their time is still true. Nothing that has happened or that can ever happen can alter the truth of it. Ireland belongs to the Irish. We believe, then, that it is the duty of Irishmen to struggle always, never giving in or growing weary, until they have won back their country again.

The object of Na Fianna Éireann is to train the boys of Ireland to fight Ireland's battle when they are men. In the past the Irish, heroically though they have struggled, have always lost, for want of discipline, for want of military knowledge, for want of plans, for want of leaders. The brave Irish who rose in '98, in '48 and in '67, went down because they were not soldiers: we hope to train Irish boys from their earliest years to be soldiers, not only to know the trade of a soldier – drilling, marching, camping, signalling, scouting and (when they are old enough) shooting – but also, what is far more important, to understand and prize military discipline and to have a military spirit. Centuries of oppression and of unsuccessful effort have almost extinguished the military spirit of Ireland: if that were once gone – if Ireland were to become a land of contented slaves – it would be very hard, perhaps impossible, ever to arouse her again.

. . . Our programme includes every element of military training. We are not mere 'Boy Scouts', although we teach and practise the art of scouting. Physical culture, infantry drill, marching, the routine of camp life, semaphore and Morse signalling, scouting in all its branches, elementary tactics, ambulance and first aid, swimming, hurling and football, all are included in our scheme of training; and opportunity is given to the older boys for bayonet and rifle practice. This does not exhaust our programme, for we believe that mental culture should go hand in hand with physical culture, and we provide instruction

174

in Irish and in Irish history, lectures on historical and literary subjects, and musical and social entertainments as opportunities permit.

. . . Is it too much to hope that after so many centuries the old ideals are still quick in the heart of Irish youth, and that this year we shall get many hundred Irish boys to come forward and help us to build up a brotherhood of young Irishmen strong of limb, true and pure in tongue and heart, chivalrous, cultured in a really Irish sense, and ready to spend themselves in the service of their country? *Sinne, Na Fianna Éireann.*

Like he said, a masterpiece.

When I finished the book I thought, language – that's his real subject, not history. Still, he'd come to the right country, the one that daily sounds out to an ancient beat the oft half-hidden intersection. His grandfather had evidently been a revered lexicographer. He let that slip in. Was anyone impressed? I doubt it. The Irish are born lexicographers. But definitions need to be examined carefully. Thomas Middlehoff gave his 'categoric support' to the Sapir-Whorf hypothesis. 'We see and hear and otherwise experience very largely as we do because the language habits of our community predispose certain choices of interpretation.' I read the sentence a few times in the hope of

175

understanding it and I thought, my God, if this theory is right it's terrifying. Language – his own – had after all given the world the speeches from which it still recoils in horror. Is language the key to everything? In the chapter 'The Irish, Language and Memory' he certainly emphasised his belief that English was key to the story of Ireland, a language that had been forced upon us and then effectively stolen by us, a sound-boomerang, which the English never caught. In the end he was too clever for me and I gave up when it came to Kant. Though I liked Kant's line about the crooked timber of humanity from which no straight thing comes – something like that. I liked it. But I disagreed with it. Strongly.

In fact, since much of the writing was not obscure exactly, but overly elliptical, he might not have alienated his miniscule readership had he not published his chapter on anti-Semitism. Our anti-Semitism – in a book by a German! We were outraged. Oh the bit about Maud Gonne's mad anti-Semitism wasn't a surprise. She was built for passionate hatred, that woman, and not for love, as Yeats found out. Not that it made any difference. He was going to love on, come what may. 'Heart! O heart! If she'd but turn her head,/ You'd know the folly of being comforted.' 'Mmm,' as May Garvey said to me once when I'd declaimed it passionately, 'Olivia, that girl's head was turned from day one.' Yes, the reprinting of an anti-Semitic poster which had been pasted around in Dublin that was 'unforgivable'. Which for a country that believes in confession and absolution is a pretty powerful statement. It was hard to believe the rubbish-leaflet had been written by an Irishman. The language lacks rhythm, though the repetition of questions has its own pseudo-Socratic power, the power if insistence:

Who is your enemy? Who has for centuries trampled you in the dust?

Who engineered the artificial famine of 1846–48 when two million of our people famished amidst plenty and which forced millions of our people into exile?

Who let loose the scum of England – the Jew Greenwood's Black and Tans – to murder, burn and loot our country?

Who is maintaining the inhuman partition of our country?

Who unceasingly endeavoured to represent us to all nations as a race of clowns and half-wits?

Who are the self-chosen 'protectors and patrons of Christianity'?

Who organised the priest hunts, despoiled our churches and even excluded His Holiness the Pope from the Peace Conference at Versailles?

Who is flooding Ireland with Jewish masonic drivel and filth, insulting our national aspirations and the Christian religion, paralysing your mind and warping your judgement?

The answer is England – Ireland's only enemy.

England's foes are Ireland's friends – may they increase and multiply!

Moladh go deo leo!

Who is persecuting and victimising our fellow countrymen in the enemy occupied area of our country?

Who has never concealed its sympathy with the German nation?

Success to Ireland's friends.

Where do you stand in the war?

Well we didn't stand anywhere, actually. We were neutral. A neutral, passionate society. That's rare. Luckily for us, others weren't – neutral, I mean. And now that it was all over we didn't want to be called in on the wrong side of that awful horror, and by a German! Not when we'd been on no one's side at all. Just our own. Because we believed, and who can blame us, that our centuries of suffering, which we knew by heart, in the literal meaning of that phrase, had absolved us of responsibility. Suffering has moral power. Carrying one's cross is a well-known mark of identification. So we didn't want to have our pathetic poster that had been written and disseminated by idiots in the thirties and forties reprinted for us. We were not anti-Semitic. We were anti-anyone who wasn't Catholic. We weren't going to persecute them. God, no. We were going to convert them, particularly in Africa. We were going to save their immortal souls for God, the Redeemer. Long tradition there. 'Anti-Semitic, Tom?' as Bogus Brogan said to my father when the book came out. 'He's a perfectly nice man, Tom, but understands nothing about this country. How could he? He's a German! And remember, Tom, even a visit to a Protestant church can lose us our immortal soul. Anti-Semitic? Protestants, Methodists, Anglicans, all inferior! What do you think, Tom? Am I being unfair here? Are we not the chosen people? Everyone else is headed for limbo. At best. So anti-Semitism? Par for the course, Tom! Catholicism, that's the only religion.' And my father and I agreed that Bogus was a mite more subversive than we'd thought.

If my father believed the book unwise, the bishop considered it more than unwise. He considered it 'dangerous' and the chess games ceased for quite some time. Anyway, the book came and went. Perhaps, since Thomas Middlehoff wanted to stay in the country with which 'he'd fallen in love', in Bridget's triumphant phrase, the book was luckily unsuccessful. There was a short interview on Radio Éireann, not a huge audience as he went out just before midnight, according to my father. No, Thomas Middlehoff wasn't headed for the *Late Late Show*. In the end it all settled down as it always

179

does. And, as they always do, in time people forgot, though forgetting is an elective process.

Mr Middlehoff 'did a bit of travelling' – not a concept we understood then, when our 'travelling' was mostly limited to emigration leavened by visits home. He returned after some time but was little seen in the town. He was, according to Bridget, who told Sally, who told my mother, 'in hibernation out in Lake House. That woman comes. That Mrs Calder. Just arrives, not very often, just a day's notice, here and gone so to say. He's like a Trappist monk after she leaves. Walking round in contemplation no doubt, but not of God I think. And Mrs Calder, she's very abrupt. No charm at all. None. And not that good-looking either. Married I'd say.' As to where 'that woman' slept when she stayed, which was rarely, no one wanted to be witness to mortal sin. Which Mr Middlehoff seemed to understand because Bridget always had the day off when Mrs Calder came and 'only saw her for a few minutes, usually accidentally'. Though it was my opinion that Bridget engineered these accidents, fascinated as we all are by those who break the rules. And seem to survive. And, of course, he was German, 'they do things differently there'. And she was? English? 'Sounds English, anyway,' according to Bridget.

Yes, his book was forgotten or ignored, which is how we get on in time, how we get over things – nations and individuals – by forgetting to remember. Even when I first read it, all those years ago, I remember wondering, was he trying to warn us? Or is that just what I wonder now? Yes, now I wonder, was he trying to warn us? Or give us absolution? Then I remembered that he probably didn't believe in absolution. We did, and absolution would become more and more essential. Though as time went on '*te absolvo*' had to be almost choked out of us.

CHAPTER 16

Although I'd left Ireland, Ireland hadn't left me. For three decades you couldn't get away from us: decades that came rushing at us in their violent reality, tumbling out of centuries of dreams. Rage grew at the savage injustice of an administration in Northern Ireland of such adamantine stupidity they knocked themselves out with it. And the rage mingled with that low mist of frustrated nationalism that, even after the riot and the arrival of the British soldiers, we'd all believed would drift into some new arrangement. What had become a lazy-hazy love dream of a United Ireland, surely it would not trap us again in the prison of conviction, in the icy palace of obsession? No, the dream would come to us. It would all come true. Over the rainbow. Over the border. Someday. We couldn't wait. We didn't.

So in those decades I came from a famous country, and when you achieve fame it's hard to give it up. The narrative was too compelling. The story of Ireland had everything. History and heroism, spectacular violence and violent spectaculars, an ever-growing cast and a chorus, as classical tragedy demands. It was a chorus of victims. We could name them, for about a week, or at least number the dead. But there were so many, so many, that eventually they all just rolled themselves up into one word, plural, 'victims', of bombs and bullets. But it was the bombs, I believe, that tore into our soul and most certainly into mine as each bomb left me feeling ill for days.

Sometimes I felt I'd turn to stone as the litany for the dead continued . . . 'Let us pray,' or not, for the three men and a bomb in Creggan in 1970, which went off too early and took the two daughters of one of them to oblivion or heaven, depending on your point of view, and for the two boys, suspects, shot dead shortly afterwards by the British Army. Suspected wrongly, as it turned out. And 'let us remember in our prayers' the three young soldiers from Ayr in Scotland – two of them brothers, seventeen and eighteen, hopelessly young, possibly drunk – who were stolen out of their bar-room trap and shot in the head on a beautiful mountain road outside Belfast, the lights of which maybe glimmered that night as they grasped in one surprised second that life, for them, was over. Amen. Was there a moon? Was there some light before they joined 'the wronged ones in the darkness', a line from *Oedipus at Colonus* that made me weep with recognition when I first heard it. Someone must know. Maybe one of the thousands of Protestants who marched to the memorial service led by the Reverend Ian Paisley, enraged and frightened and calling for internment. 'Now! Now! Before these men can commit any more atrocities.' No one had much patience with the idea of building a case. 'Wasn't it as clear as ditchwater,' a fascinating phrase, 'that *only* internment would work?' And the Provos, newly created in the dawn of the seventies, the Provisional IRA, 'a nomenclature of almost oriental obfuscation,' as Bogus said, sensing that they had a very short time indeed before evidence in a real court of law might rob them of their leaders, bombed on, provocatively. Banking on the oft-proved stupidity of their enemy, the cast-iron stupidity that did indeed sleep-walk a government into the trap of internment as the number of bombings and casualties increased. April 1971, thirty-seven dead; May, forty-seven; July, ninety-one. It worked! On 9 August 1971 internment was introduced. And we watched in despair as the great recruiting officer as they call him, whose image alone as he tore a man from his family and locked him up without trial, concentrated hearts and minds all right. But whose? 'How could they be so stupid?' Bogus, in a fury when I was back for a few days. And he was right. Even moderates walked out of assemblies. 'A moderate after all is not always entitled to moderation, Olivia.' And within a month the number of bombings rose to nearly two hundred. We would, in a sense, 'make Northern Ireland ungovernable as a first step to achieving a United Ireland'. It's a technique. One which we

184

would teach the world. After all, we're natural teachers.

And a man who for a time had only ever come out at night, and even then, bearded, would be soon became our headmaster – a long tenure.

I was with English friends in Chichester in Sussex, in rehearsals for *Six Characters in Search of an Author* when, in truth, our thirty-year war began, at a peace march. Sunday 30 January 1972, that Bloody Sunday when thirteen men were massacred, seventeen wounded – one, it turned out later, fatally – by the British Army. And the image of a priest tending the dying and the dead and whispering to them last-minute hopes of forgiveness and eternal salvation wrapped its way around the world and around hearts that had perhaps grown a trifle weary of the weight of that long-awaited dream, United Ireland. Now the world wept with us and that priest's handkerchief waving in the wind became as fierce a symbol as Delacroix's torch. It seemed that the cause came to triumphant life as sympathy and outrage at our suffering swept over us and 'the captive voice', *an glon gafa*, soared and would never be drowned again. Stormont, that 'Protestant parliament for a Protestant state', fell. And quickly. In March 1972. The dream was within our grasp. It was ours for the taking. How could we lose it now? Bloody Friday, 21 July 1972, when the Provisionals detonated twenty car bombs in Belfast, killing nine and injuring 130. Bodies and parts of bodies were gathered up sometimes in the hope of identification and, sometimes, in the hope of resurrection.

Is there resurrection without identification? It's a question of faith. Which itself became shaky as the horrors continued. 'Oh God, Olivia . . . twenty-one killed in Birmingham, bombs in bars!' 'The Miami Showband! A band, for God's sake. A band!' Bayardo Bar on the Shankhill Road, five dead. La Mon restaurant – twelve burned alive. 'We need no sermons any more on the flames of hell.' I was in a bar with Bogus on 27 August 1979 when Lord Mountbatten, his teenage grandson and a local boy were murdered in their boat, which was 'blown to smithereens'. We said nothing. No one said anything. We were about to go home when news of Warrenpoint came in. Eighteen soldiers killed in a double bombing. The ones who escaped the first got the second. 'The sheer expertise of it,' said Bogus. Expertise? Well up to a point. Because it was accidentally that the IRA discovered the car bomb, though it lost its Quartermaster General, accidentally. 'Since "the black stuff", an essential, is based on fertiliser, of which you could say we have plenty, Olivia, the stuff could travel anywhere. We were further rewarded by the land mine.'

So we hauled ourselves in agony through the eighties: Hyde Park. Cavalry, bandsmen and horses, and the mangling and mingling of bodies; the Droppin' Well Bar in Ballykelly where seventeen dropped into oblivion. Two children included in the list of the dead, 'Shouldn't have been there, I suppose.' Bogus, bitter again. Then Brighton, followed by the IRA statement of disappointment that only five died and that the Prime Minister survived. Remembrance Sunday, eleven civilians buried in rubble in the Poppy Day Massacre. 'Wrong memory, clearly, Olivia.' The next year, 1988, six soldiers killed by a bomb on a minibus, Lisburn, and eight killed in Ballygawley. To bring the decade to a close, eleven soldiers killed in Deal in Kent. And the nineties? Warrington, 1993, when three-year-old Johnathan Ball and twelve-year-old Tim Parry 'took the blast, as they say, Olivia – a Saturday afternoon shopping trip!' Then, Omagh, 1998. Saturday again, twenty-nine killed by the Real IRA, which, as Bogus said, was 'a reality check for us all'. As indeed it was.

And I began to wonder, were we breeding aristocrats of terror and teaching the world that the age of deference is not dead? Though fear is a great leveller of the populace a noble cause raises the perpetrator above the common fray. And we had a noble cause. We had that lovely history dripping in heroes. But 'our boys' were now giving a hideous twist to that story. The UVF and the British Army, of course their atrocities shocked us but they were capable, 'that tribe', of anything. Oh yes, you could expect anything, any horror from them. But our saintly ghosts, were their names now called our in benediction for deeds they'd never dreamed of? Named as heroic precursors of this? Of bombing civilians? Sarsfield, Wolfe Tone, precursors of this? Patrick Pearse, who when he marched out of the GPO in order to spare civilians must have known what awaited him. Was he also a precursor? My first love? The way you love purity and sacrifice in a hero, when you're about twelve, when being a nun and being a soldier for Ireland got somehow mixed up with being a religious martyr, preserving purity of body and purity of soul for love of God and for love of country, dreaming once of being laid out in my confirmation dress and veil in my coffin, the whole town in awe of my heroism. And I began to ask myself why that lovely country of mine, which had preached such reverence for the body, such passionate belief that it should be sent back whole, such determination that its sexual power be used for procreation, not just for pleasure; how could such a country have found the destruction of the body in such a savage way, not exactly acceptable, perhaps, but a way of understanding it? Is there, I began to wonder, a connection? That those who see in the body the source of all sin might find it more acceptable to blow it to kingdom come? Which of course never comes. Or does it?

And if I was bewildered through those decades, totally bewildered, so was the country I came from. The majority, what was the phrase? 'Condemn utterly what is happening, this barbarity.' But that's all we did. Condemn. And march. But not often enough. Was it the roll-call of the heroic dead that gave the impression we'd granted absolution to those fighting for the great old cause, though not quite in the manner we'd imagined? Did the dead stop us from bringing the South to a total standstill? To say, as they say nowadays, 'not in my name'. Maybe it's hard to reject such a determined suitor, hard to reject someone who wants to be united with you so much in holy conjunction that they'll kill their way to get to you. And as Bogus said to my mother, and it made her laugh, 'Shotgun marriages have their own romance.' Yes, sometimes we laughed at the black bitterness that lay beneath his vanity, which remained strong. Because even in those dark days Bogus would boast of the success of his collection of witticisms, poetry and stories, *How to be Irish*, subtitle: 'The Lessons are Easy – It's the Homework that's Hard'.

It was. It took thirty years for us to learn our lessons. No one thought it would last that long. Why not? We'd been preparing our minds for it, but above all our hearts. And if it doesn't start there, in the heart, it doesn't start anywhere.

CHAPTER 17

As I remember in those early years of atrocities, when I talked to my mother I was careful with language. Was she all right? And each time, though sad, very sad, she was also calm. Completely calm. Is it an act? Yes? No? and I'd concentrate on every movement of her voice up and down the scale, listening, alert and fearful of hearing a note that was too low or one that might soar too swiftly and too quickly and fall again, and me not there to catch it. She was, however, utterly calm. She was utterly cold. And she was utterly contemptuous. Which was not her style. 'Who are these people?' she'd ask. 'Did we make them? How?' And once, when she handed the phone to him, and I remember this, 'There'll be more. There always has been, to make up to the dead,' he said. He was right about that.

Sometimes, however, we didn't strike the right note with each other. But we did well enough. We developed a technique and taught ourselves to briefly acknowledge the fact of the latest 'brutality, terrible, terrible' and then to talk about the universe. Our universe, a backwash to the life I lived. We'd talk through the years of Mrs Brannigan's boys, who'd joined the bank as she'd hoped, and of her certainty that Adrian would someday be made an assistant bank manager and of how May Garvey's longed-for son, now a teenager, had told his mother he might have a vocation, might go to Maynooth to study for the priesthood, 'back to where he came from, my miracle boy'. And we had many more than the three or four families to whom Miss Austen bore witness but our background noise was more, much more fierce. Miss Austen kept the sound of battle off-stage. We couldn't quite do that. But we did OK. And of course we talked of the life I lived, of the life I do not talk of here and of how grateful I was, of how I was more than grateful. And she'd sometimes remind me that she always knew that the years she felt I'd sacrificed, which was not how I ever saw it, would come back to me. And we agreed that they had. 'You are,' she'd say to me, 'living now that great blessing, a private life of love.' And I liked the phrase then and I still do.

So maybe I'd relaxed about them and began to feel confident that their souls and hearts were mended. That they had been darned up by the invisible thread of love, by minute-by-minute stitching through the hours of days. But perhaps the mending process had been too exhausting because though they had many years together he died younger than we'd all expected and long before her. His dying took a few weeks. I came home, of course. Sat by his side. With her. And once, when he knew there was no chance, I thought that he seemed to be trying to speed things up a bit to save her the anguish. But maybe I'm wrong. Still, there was a note in his voice one day when he whispered to me, after I said she looked tired, 'I'm doing my best,' and later I wondered, doing your best at what? And I'm still not certain. That man would have hurried up his dying if he thought it might have helped her.

And though I sat there in the first week or so they didn't need me, perhaps didn't really want me. So I'd go for long walks knowing they had private work to do. Especially him. He was setting her up for life without him. No one thought she could live it but he set her up for the journey. And, this will be no surprise, they talked non-stop in those last weeks. I'd leave them in the hospital to give them some more time together, which amazingly was all they wanted, more time together. After a lifetime together they wanted more time. And that's love, I suppose. The nurse told me that one night he'd called out in panic, 'My God, I'm dying. I'm dying!' She shouldn't have told me. I still can't bear to think about it. But he rallied past the fear because the next day he greeted us with smiles and little jokes, they set about their whispering again and because it was raining I sat in the corridor reading Eliot and

Henry James. The constriction of language and its expansion, a rhythm, like that of the heart. But his was weak and getting weaker. Then, about a week after that night-time outburst, at four in the afternoon, one Thursday afternoon, when he'd insisted we pop out for a walk, he left us. He left us with the silence of his heart and his heart had been a most beautiful thing. He left us, as you would expect, before we got back from that last walk of ours with the still-living dream of him. Perhaps he was trying to save her. Not to make her witness to his last moments. And that's love, I suppose. But up until that day the conversation, that long love-poem, two people talking through life, that continued. And that's love, I suppose.

Everyone came to the funeral. Everyone. Including Thomas Middlehoff, which was nice of him though some people were uneasy to see him there. He was more than the German now. He was a German with an Irish history. He was writing about us still and at a delicate time. Theft. The German, Wittgenstein, might indeed have visited us and written about us but that was different. 'Didn't Dev invite him to Ireland? Dev was mad about sums and didn't we offer him nationality when he was in trouble, being a Jew? But we're not a nation of mathematicians. Saints and scholars, yes, but no good at sums. Though we will get better in time.' Bogus, another letter. And though Heinrich Böll's *Irish Journal* had been noted decades before, we're a well-read nation and words obsess us, whether on the page or on the wind. We also knew Böll was a Catholic and *The Lost Honour of Katharina Blum* had had quite a bit of success in a country where such a title would resonate. Böll told us things we had wanted to hear, though there is an under-note. But Thomas Middlehoff! No prizes for him. Still, he'd 'done no real harm' so they 'let it go', that day at the funeral.

I was really touched that he came. Afterwards he shook hands with my mother, bowed, talked about how he'd felt there'd been a deep bond with my father and that he would 'greatly miss him'. She made no response to that. Then he turned to me, 'Olivia,' a handshake and bow and suddenly he bent down and gave me a little kiss. My mother looked away. It probably seemed inappropriate but it wasn't. Not at all. I nearly put my arms out to hold him or maybe hold on to him because I felt he understood things better than most. But I didn't. Still, the moment lodged with me and I felt I had to see him again before I left. So a few days later, when my mother sat with her sisters talking over old times, times I didn't know, when they were young, I drove out to see him. Patricia, Bridget's daughter, who for three days a week worked as his secretary, said he'd be alone. It was a Sunday. He wasn't. I should have rung. A tall, thin woman opened the door.

'Who is it, Harriet?'

'I've no idea,' she called back to him and before I had a chance to introduce myself to her he was standing before me. He looked shocked, not embarrassed exactly but perhaps a little angry. I stumbled over myself, apologies falling from my lips, a veritable confetti of 'I'm sorry'.

'Please stop apologising. Come in. We're not in flagrante, you know.'

And he almost hooted his laughter and I never saw a man who looked at a woman with such adoration, except one, or two.

'Olivia . . . O'Hara. I'm sorry, Olivia, I do not know your married name. May I introduce Mrs Calder, Harriet Calder.'

He seemed preoccupied and clearly unhappy I was there. I apologised again and again. She stopped me.

'Come in,' she said.

He looked angrily at her. But she was insistent. As though she needed my presence for some reason. She had what they call natural authority. I followed this woman, Mrs Calder, as she strode down the hall so fast I cursed the stupid shoes I was wearing and felt inelegant and irritated and all out-of-kilter in that house.

'Drink?' asked Harriet Calder and then she yawned slightly. And a shadow of deep exhaustion passed over her face. And then I noticed that her face was very thin and bony. Maybe more than just thin and bony. And then I saw that she was pale. And maybe more than pale. And I looked away and I told myself, don't react. Compose yourself. Compose your face.

'Harriet! It's not yet midday! What will Olivia think of us?' As if she gave a damn.

'Yes please,' I said. 'Whiskey.'

And Harriet Calder smiled. A strange, crooked smile. But I knew enough about a slight distortion of features to know they have the power to trap a man. The things you learn!

'That settles it Thomas. Scotch all right? Thomas prefers Irish whiskey. Are you patriotic?'

'Scotch is fine,' I said.

'Not patriotic then? Thank God.'

I looked around the dark wood-panelled room, smoky velvet curtains and in the corner a deep winged chair in which you could almost hide. He motioned me to a low sofa with colours of old gold and dark green stitched into a pattern I couldn't decipher and awkwardly I sat down and tried to balance my drink, too tense to stretch out to the small side table. All in all, I did not feel at home, and neither of them would ever have issued that old invitation, 'come in and make yourself at home'. But after a while I realised I wanted to be there. Very much. Yes, I wanted to be in the darkened room that smelled of old velvets and of old books – no paperbacks, I noted – and of old wood. Because in all the heaviness in the darkened room I could feel the energy, the restless, thrilling energy. Sexual. Impossible to miss. Then they started speaking again. And though they spoke perfect English I felt I was listening to foreigners, that the rhythms were different. I knew I was almost out of my depth but I believe in hanging on, and I hung on to the words that day.

'Olivia came home for her father's funeral – Tom O'Hara.'

'Doesn't everyone?' she asked. He looked away. She was not the kind of woman you could apologise for. And he didn't.

'Mr O'Hara? Wasn't he the man who returned the gate?'

'Yes.'

'And the father, therefore, of the boy? You gave them the gate.'

'Yes.'

She looked at me and said, 'Thomas liked your father. Never liked his own. You live in London?'

'Yes.'

'With your husband?'

'Harriet!'

She laughed. 'It's a perfectly natural question.'

'Of course,' I said.

'Children?'

I nodded. She was not interested in pursuing the question further.

'Thomas's son died. Frederick. And another child. Did he tell you that?'

'No.'

'Indeed! Thomas is a very careful man and I am a careless woman.'

'Not true, Harriet. Not true.'

And she silenced him with a look. Power. She had power. Then she smiled again.

'However I have some caring instincts and I must now leave Thomas at a moment when I have given him bad news. I am pleased you are here with him. An unexpected but welcome visitor. Stay a little, while he bids me goodbye in private.'

I nodded. And she motioned to him to follow her. And he did. I would guess he always obeyed and anyway, I thought it was clearly too late for rebellion. Perhaps she's right and he needs me. I owe him from long ago. I picked up a book, a copy of which was open on the desk, lines about goodness. How rare it is. Hardly an insight. Had he been reading it to her? When he came back he poured himself another drink. He looked at me as though he trusted me and I felt peculiarly proud.

'She's dying!' he said. 'Harriet Calder is dying!' and he laughed, that strange violent laugh I'd heard earlier. 'Incredible! Incredible! She is the love of my life and she's dying. She's dying.' He was almost shouting as he paced the room. 'Sorry,' he said. 'Sorry.' But he couldn't stop. It was unstoppable this drumming out of rage at this outrage by the gods. Carry on, I thought. We both know it will make no difference. And he did continue, the fast, staccato drumming, drumming it all out of himself with useless words.

'Do you know what that means? Do you really know what it means? What I am facing? She is finally leaving me, the love of my life.'

'I do,' I whispered.

He leaned for a moment on the back of that winged chair as if to draw breath, and then more words, faster, which did not suit the rhythm of his voice, which was designed for slower, more controlled speech. I wished he'd stop. I realised I had held him in such high regard that I wanted him to be someone who suffered silently. Who could imply the things he knew, not spell them out for me. I had allocated a part to him. He wasn't playing it. I didn't want passionate incoherence from this man. That was something I could do for myself. No, I wanted dignified silence with a hint of something underneath, something that implied there was an answer. That was the kind of silence I wanted. Then I wondered, what have I come for? What am I looking for here? Away from my own life and back in the one I left? Back for a funeral. And I looked hard at him, willing him to think of me and what I'd just been through. But he seemed lost in his own recollections. We all have our favourite scene. No, not favourite, essential. He was lost in something, gazing at something or somewhere he'd been once and, as 'that man, Yeats' told us, if you get to know that scene, that one lifescene, you will know the man. Where was he? What was he looking at? Who was he looking at? Then he took a deep breath, as though that whispered affirmation of a few moments ago convinced him he was not mad.

'Good. Good. Yes. You know, of course you know what I'm going through. Harriet Calder is dying. Incredible. I know that woman. I know her. Can you say that about anyone and be certain?'

'Yes.'

'The first time I made love to Harriet Calder was the first time I made love.'

I gasped. I was being attacked. I was being invaded by this uninvited intimacy. How dare he! I looked around as though looking for escape. How dare he do this to me. But there was no possibility of stopping him . . . of stopping this . . . this what? This savagery. Not now. And though he said, 'Forgive me,' it was contemptible special pleading.

'Forgive me. Forgive me, Olivia. Unpardonable. Obsession. The universe reduced to one – the universe lit by one. Madness. Is that the perversion of love? Hearts with one purpose alone . . . seem enchanted to a stone . . . Is that not the line?'

'Yes,' I said, 'but Yeats was speaking of love of country.'

And I wondered as I said it, does all love spring from the same source? Can all loves be diverted or twisted? What is it that makes a love flow kindly on? Who or what decides?

'Harriet and I had a son.'

Please don't tell me this! We are not close friends. That's what I wanted to say. But I didn't. I suppose the secret soul of a man is eternally seductive.

'We had a son, though I did not know of this until it was too late. How could I? War swallows up all the normal rhythms. I must have another drink.'

I saw my opportunity: 'I don't know why I came and I'm incredibly sorry and . . . and I must go. I'm sorry.'

And I made an inelegant effort to rise from that uncomfortably low sofa.

'Please do not, Olivia. Please do not go. I do not normally make requests and only with Harriet do I beg.'

I looked away. And then I remembered that my father had told me of the long-ago conversation that he'd had with this man. 'A man of some particular understanding, Olivia.' And I remembered the gate. Would Dada want me to stay? Oh Dada, should I stay? Oh Dada, where are you? This man seems in agony. I sat down again. As my father would have done. Thomas Middlehoff continued to pace around. I know that necessity.

'I . . . received a letter from Munich, dated the fourth of July 1944. It read like a love letter. A love letter from Harriet is a most unusual matter. If I'd died that day, and so many did, I felt I would have died happy. That was but a momentary feeling. It was followed by an urgent, overwhelming desire to see her, which of course

201

was not possible. I had been wounded and was in hospital. On the eighteenth of July, for three solid hours, Munich was bombed. Hamburg, we'd hoped, would be the end of summer bombings. Hamburg, August 1943. Two hundred thousand dead in Hamburg they said. In Munich? How many? Was *she* dead was all I wanted to know. *Was she* dead? Millions die and we are so designed that we are broken only by the death of those we love. The others are lost in history. We are not good. It's the self, always the self. *Was she* dead? I left the hospital where I was being quickly made whole again in order to be sent back to fight. I cannot even remember how I managed to get out of this. I was heedless of the risk I was taking in "so undermining the morale of the armed forces". Absent. I searched for her. I searched for her knowing that if I saw her I would live. I would be triumphant.

A victor in the land of the defeated. I knew I would have pulled what made life bearable, my life bearable, from that place. I would rejoice in a city in which others had perished. Where others had died, sucked down in melted asphalt, no way to drown. Others had been incinerated, made into ashes in a second. Gone. Some had been shrunken into compact completeness. Men no bigger than children. I will stop. The rushing roar of the thing was over when I got there. It was quiet. Shock, at its most profound, is silent. It is the silence that seems to stop time. Many, I saw, were smiling. Real smiles. Real radiance. Until you saw their eyes and you knew they were now mad. And some were truly elegant. Yes, elegantly picking their way as ball-gowned ladies and the formally dressed men who guide them do as they cross a courtyard to the sound of music, carefully judging the position of each foot in case they slip and fall. And one figure seemed to me to be of particular elegance. That's how she appeared to me. A woman of particular elegance. Elongated. A Modigliani figure. Behold the woman!

'Behold Harriet. Hare-ee-et, the name means home-ruler in German – God! The Harriet that only I know. That Harriet before she made herself Harriet Calder, and however she remakes herself she will always be that Harriet to me. But the future was impossible to imagine that day as I moved, and I moved quickly, quickly, though I did not run towards her, remembering her contempt for obvious signs of my desperation. She stood quietly watching a number of men carefully place parts of bodies in a sack. She seemed lost in contemplation of them. She was carrying a suitcase. I whispered, "Harriet," as though it were the most natural thing in the world to sound out her name softly in a steaming broken street where many who had choked to death lay around. "Harriet?" She did not acknowledge me. Then I put my hand out to carry the suitcase. She pulled it closer to her as though I were a thief. I tried again and she blazed out at me as though she would burn me with hatred. I stepped back. I almost tripped on pieces of masonry. She did not respond. If I'd fallen I think she would have simply stepped over me and walked on. Then I knew. I'd heard rumours, after Hamburg. Rumours of mothers, husbands, wives, who hid in suitcases the bodies of those they loved, who had been shrunken to a mummified state. I looked at her, the shape of her. Elongated. It was over, her pregnancy. My father had told me deliberately late. And she had not told me at all. Eight months. She had not told me. "Give it to me," I said. She shook her head. "Give it to me!" She nodded. Such unfamiliar acquiescence. "Wait," she said.

"'You must wait, Thomas." And I did. For many hours. Finally she put the suitcase down on the ground. It was between us. I picked it up. It was very light. One hand was sufficient. Within my other hand I held hers. There was nothing haunting or romantic about it. Just a determination not to let her go. We said nothing. We made our way to the station and got off the train at the first stop, walked and walked in silence until finally she said "Here". We did not make any mark. It was unnecessary. We would remember. It was a common tale of the time in my country but not much told. Who would listen? No one. Why should they? But many of us did not know that at the time. I learned earlier than most. In the winter semester of 1945–46 I heard Karl Jaspers' lecture,

"Die Schuldfrage" and I began to understand that it was not only the war that we had lost. We had lost our individual moral responsibility. Each and every one of us was now impure, each marked with national disgrace. We were now a tribe. We bore the yoke. This was our story now. Perhaps we would never have another. The irony! Jaspers was the first to address publicly the question of German guilt. Listening to him, I knew our private stories of grief and suffering would, and should, never be told. We would have to bury them. We would have to bury each and every individual story within the horror story of our time in history. Few accepted such a concept then. The other students were not disruptive that day, but they were angry as they listened to Jaspers, the first to tell us the truth and therefore condemned as brutal. It would be years before the Eichmann Trial, when the final uncovering and the unveiling of the nakedness of it all would roll out before our eyes and those of the world. We'd blinded ourselves before. Guilt blinds, which is why we will always understand Oedipus better than Medea. Maybe, deep down, Oedipus always knew. What do you think?'

I was exhausted. I thought nothing except, I am too tired for this. Where are you Dada? Help me, Dada. But there was no respite. He sat down opposite me. He had to continue, I could see that, and with a sigh I realised I was the designated listener. And one, it would seem, who had a duty.

'. . .She stole away from me within days. No address. Nothing. How did I find her? When she had remade herself. When she had made a new life and buried the old. So that she could be subsumed into something, anything, that was not what she'd been before. To build new memories. So Harriet, with her then adequate English, which quickly became perfect, her compelling presence and that emotional carelessness which men who wish to be hurt find essential, married an Englishman. She washed herself clean in the river of an infinitely more appealing history, that of Henry Calder and the country he came from. Henry Calder with whom she had two children, Barty and Hugh. I am surprised you have not heard of her. She moves in different circles, perhaps?'

I remain silent. I knew the circles, though I did not know her.

'She is well-known for her charity work and her many affairs, which though they cause me exquisite pain have been irrelevant to my obsession. I too married. Veronika, the daughter of my father's oldest friend. And I too had a son, Frederick. Who also died. He was a delicate child, as you would call him here. He contracted meningitis quite suddenly, over less than forty-eight hours it stole him away. I told myself his immune system was low after flu. My father, however, did not allow me this defence: "Your son did not fight hard enough for life. He gave up. You harmed your son when you harmed his mother. You have brought

206

catastrophe on your life. You have lost your son and you have destroyed Veronika." He was right. The damage one can cause to others in a single private lifetime. I could not stay away from Harriet, a woman who would not stay with me. Veronika made a number of hopeless suicide attempts. Hopeless because they were cries for help to a man who was deaf, who had no interest in the extreme devotion of a woman to whom he was not devoted. That is the horror of obsession. The heart, as your Mr Yeats says, "enchanted to a stone".'

And I thought, why does he keep misinterpreting that line? It's about country, obsessive love of country. Or is he right?

'My father, who was not a puritan, nevertheless regarded marriage as a particular territory that must be guarded. I had failed. Failed in the subterfuge that would have created for my wife Veronika an acceptable illusion. "You are contemptible," he informed me. I had in a sense been asleep on duty. He convinced himself that watching his mother in her agony and her rage, her explosive hatred of Harriet, had made holding on to life not appealing to Frederick. Yes. Just that: not appealing. And life must be made to seem appealing to children.'

And I thought, he's right. That's the job. He sighed and leaned back in his armchair. And then he smiled and I almost smiled back in relief. It must nearly be over. I will be able to get away soon.

'How strange, Olivia, Henry will look after her. In the last months. He'll have her in the end. At the end.'

'Henry?'

'Her husband, Henry.'

'Ah, yes.'

What else could I say? Though for a second I wondered, had Harriet just given him a story? The one he needed for survival. Did he ever think there might be another version? Maybe Henry's? But he wasn't interested in Henry's story. He'd got the story of his own life. It was probably too late to change it now.

'She is leaving. She is leaving both of us.'

Which was a way of putting it. He downed his whiskey quickly and looked at me as though he hoped I would do the same. Yes, it was over. The confession, for that's what it had been, was over. I had no power to dispense penance or grant absolution. And suddenly, instead of relief, I felt sad. He had let me know him, which is rare in life.

'I am in a state of shock, Olivia. Forgive me. Please. I thought I would never feel such shock again.'

'I'm in a state of shock myself. And I must now get back to my mother.'

He stood up.

'I realise that I have behaved terribly. I am so sorry. My father would tell you my moral nature has been exposed again and is again less than impressive. You are in mourning also. Again, I am sorry.'

I touched his hand in sympathy and we walked towards the front door. He was a cultivated man with impeccable manners, and he walked me to my car. As he opened the car door for me he said, 'Your mother reminds me of Harriet.' I was furious. How could he say that? How could he insult me like that? My mother bore no resemblance to that tall, sophisticated, probably vicious woman who was now dying.

'Yes. Yes,' he continued, as though the thought had just occurred to him and he was anxious to communicate it to me. 'To me she resembles Harriet. Your father, of course, was a man capable of the outer reaches of another kind of love. Where the self dies.'

How dare he! My father, my mother. Do not appropriate them. Not to your version of what? Love? Yes. But twisted. Theirs had been what is truest, what is best. It seemed demeaning to their story that he would try to trace within it the pattern of his own suffering. I must get away from him. And get away, back to my real home which was no longer in this country. Let him stay here. This stranger. 'The German' as we used to call him. How quickly it comes back when one is wounded. Prejudice! I must have looked angry or cold or something because as he made to close the door he said softly, as though it were a peace offering, 'I will send you a copy of my new book.

It's a collection of essays. It will be published shortly.'

'Thank you,' I said. Though I didn't mean it. I left him. I went back to her, to my mother. To beg her to come back with me. 'And leave them?' she said. 'Living close, Olivia. He was right.' I nodded. But I tried again. And again. Nothing worked.

She stayed with them.

CHAPTER 18

Thomas Middlehoff was the kind of man who, if he said he would do something, did it. Not always reassuring. A month or so later it arrived, *Connections*. It wove a theme, I suppose: the power of poets, playwrights, literary polemicists in the creation of the concept of nationality. Not exactly bestseller material. There was an essay that quoted Pearse's Christmas Day letter from St Enda's College 1915, which was destined to be his last Christmas:

> Here be ghosts that I have raised this Christmastide, ghosts of dead men that have bequeathed to us living men. Ghosts are troublesome things in a house or in a family, as we knew even before Ibsen taught us. There is only one way to appease a ghost. You must do the thing it asks you. The ghosts of a nation sometimes ask very big things; and they must be appeased, whatever the cost.
>
> Of the shade of the Norwegian dramatist

I beg forgiveness for a plagiaristic, but inevitable title.

Pearse could write. No doubt about that. Then an entire essay on Ibsen – the 'smallness' of his characters as Yeats saw it. Well, Cathleen Ní Houlihan is a presence that takes some beating on the stage, or in life. The piece on Shelley's 'Address to the Irish People' which advocated 'habits of Sobriety, Regularity and Thought' seemed a bit perverse considering Shelley ran off with two sixteen-year-olds. Not our kind of hero. The best of the eight essays was the one on Gottfried Benn, the older Benn as he'd dealt with the younger one before – twice. It was titled 'Memory: A Moral Arena'. He quoted Benn's introduction to *World of Expression*:

. . . As an example of this generation I mention my family: three of my brothers died in battle; a fourth was wounded twice; the remainder, totally bombed out, lost everything. A first cousin died at the Somme, his only son in the recent war; of that branch of the family nothing is left. I myself went to war as a doctor, 1914–18 and 1939–45. My wife died in 1945 in direct consequence of military operations. This brief summary should be about average for a fairly large German family's lot in the first half of the twentieth century.

Revisionist? Maybe. But he was right about what he'd said that day about guilt, when it had all poured out of him, the flood of words released by the shock of Harriet Calder's illness. However, sympathy for individual human suffering depends on where you came from, what the narrative is, the language you use, and, if you're German, 'I wouldn't start from here', as the Irish say. Though no guidance is provided as to an ideal starting point: 'that'd be telling'. Besides, victimhood was becoming a much fought-over territory and Germany had zero chance of carving out a single inch of it. Now I realise Thomas Middlehoff was ahead of his time. Ahead of his countryman Günter Grass, Nobel Prize-winner, who did try much later, with *Crabwalk*, to claim rather more than an inch of victimhood for his nation, yet ruined it all with his late acknowledgement (very late, on the edge of eternity really) that, as a teenager, he'd been in the SS. And admitted he'd lied about it for decades. Done more than lied. Made an issue of his contempt for others who'd joined up. Front-page news. He'd been 'in denial', as we say. A old man does not have the years to make up for sin. *Peeling the Onion* is as tearful an exercise at eighty as at eight. Though they say onions clean the blood and clear the head.

I wrote to Thomas Middlehoff, the kind of letter that says everything a writer wants to hear and never believes. He wrote back to say he'd be in

London a month or so later. I wondered if he was going to see Harriet Calder, maybe for the last time. And then I thought probably not. She would not be a woman for a long drawn-out goodbye. He was addressing a German Cultural Society at the Embassy. Would I like to attend? I said yes. Immediately. It was an impressive event. You could feel the wealth of knowledge and the weight of money, much of it old, which, whatever they say, is different. Old money. You can tell, always, as the scent of old money drifts, even in private houses, above the hum of conversation in the high-ceilinged rooms as the curtains almost whisper-kiss the floor. That night in the Embassy the muted glories of the tapestries showed war and death in softest blues and fading greens and seemed the perfect backdrop to this cast, cultured, rich and still quite careful. They would not say much out of place. His speech, hesitantly spoken, developed his essay 'The Morality of Memory', an elucidation of its weight, both personal and national. It was his theme. Few of us have more than one. The speech was structured; he posed the questions, gave the answers. Not as reliable a method as one might think.

'Memory, ladies and gentlemen. Do we live with it? Exploit it? Or kill it? Do we do this individually or collectively? In post-war Europe the choice for Germany was made for us. Germany did not choose to remember. It was forced not to forget. The phrase "Inner Emigration" I owe to Mr Buchholz – it allowed us to individually retreat from knowledge during the War. However we have now for many decades bowed our heads collectively. The Japanese, also defeated, occupy morally an altogether different position in world infamy, at least in the West where there seems to be a form of acceptance of the concept of cruelty with honour. It is clear that the Japanese believed, indeed to some extent still believe, that fierce concepts of honour bestow moral absolution without the need for confession. It is interesting to note that trials for atrocities in war were never held in Japanese courts. We, on the other hand, were condemned at home. *Heimat* and horror. With which we live. We are right. Other societies in Europe were allowed a choice. Suppression takes many forms: it is a question of cultural consciousness. The French chose suppression of their modern memory of the last war lest it sully their brave and glorious earlier past. Reluctantly they allow a few irrefutable facts to filter through. The Italians embroider so beautifully that only with difficulty can one discern the original pattern. Collusion is required to maintain this position. It is a very short time ago indeed in these societies that even a small acknowledgement of past sins has been made. It was not welcome. It never will be. The weapon of memory, turned on the self, is an apocalyptic sword.

'The weapon of memory turned on one's enemies through the power of language, however, gleams like a sword of honour. No country has wielded it with more skill than my elective home country, my Irish *Heimat*. Each home has woven into a word-tapestry of dead heroes and their wounds a perpetual stigmata.

'The glory of the ghost is little understood and its power continually misunderstood. Not here. Hamlet gave his father's ghost what he asked for. Was his father's ghost appeased? The lives of all who had survived him, who had loved him joined him in the grave. This is the victory of ghosts.'

There was polite applause. We, a small gathering, dispersed. I went up to congratulate him.

'Olivia! Olivia O'Hara. My dear.' He kissed me formally, on both cheeks. As he bent towards me I lowered my eyes, embarrassed almost by the deterioration, the strange falling in of his face that age had wrought. Or was Harriet Calder's foreshadowed death draining life from him? And then I thought, when she dies he will most likely give up on life. She will be a powerful, seductive ghost. He might be closer to eternity than I'd imagined. Then another thought possessed me: what if I never talked to him again? Ever.

'Thomas?'

'Yes, my dear friend?'

Was I a dear friend? Who knows? Then I blurted it out.

'What about the gate?'

And I realised in that moment that I had not been aware of how troubled I had been. Lost in other longings, I suppose.

'Ah, the gate.'

'Yes, Thomas, I must know.' Ruthless.

'Must, Olivia? Why? So long ago, Olivia. Such a relatively minor matter.'

'Why did you give it to my father?'

'He needed it.'

'And my mother sent it back.'

'Eventually.'

'The gate, Thomas? Where did it come from?'

We looked at each other; each of us was sad. In the end there would always be a question. Which was just sad. He bowed his head.

'Dear Olivia, must every German gate have opened on to horror?'

'I don't know. And that's the truth. For a number of years it opened on to the place . . .'

'Your father wished for the gate because your brother loved it.'

I wanted to say, that is not an answer. But I just said 'And?' Which again was brutal, I suppose.

'We do a lot for those who are dead and whom we loved. To appease a ghost, Olivia. Remember?'

Then someone came up to talk to him, a woman. She said she was a friend of Harriet Calder. At the mention of her name, or was it just out of good manners, he bowed and said how much he wished to speak to her – Ilsa, I think I heard that right – but would she excuse him for one moment as he needed to arrange something with me, and he took me a little to one side and held his hand out to me.

'Not here, Olivia. I must now talk to those who so kindly came to listen to me. Shall we meet tomorrow?'

'Yes.'

'Your house? My hotel?'

And I didn't want to let him into my life. It was too beautiful. Which was ungenerous of me.

'Your hotel. We're in the midst of reconstruction,' I lied.

He smiled at the word.

'Reconstruction takes much time. It is exhausting.'

'Yes,' I said. 'It is.'

'I'm going to Sotheby's tomorrow. There is an Irish sale there. I am particularly interested in a painting by Jack Yeats.'

I'd forgotten that he was so rich. Old money.

'Perhaps we could have lunch afterwards?'

He rang the next morning and cancelled.

'I'm not very well, Olivia. I return to Ireland. I will write. Goodbye.'

A few days later the letter arrived.

Dearest Olivia,

It is clear to me that through a small act of kindness a very long time ago a troubling question remains over a place of veneration for you, the entrance to the ground on which the central tragic event of your life took place. A strange description but one that sounds correct to me.

Did the history of this gate desecrate the place? Were the shadows that it cast in summer or winter unworthy of the landscape? Was a memory so precious to you defiled during the years your mother allowed it to stay there? You must judge. You must make the decision.

The gate opened onto a house outside Munich which swung closed on our family for a time during the war. It was used for the purpose of *Lebensborn*. *Lebensborn* means 'fount of life' – some translate it as 'source of life' – and was ironically a child welfare programme initiated by Himmler to aid the racial heredity of the Third Reich. Pregnant wives of SS officers and unmarried pregnant young women were cared for there, prior to and after birth. Much controversy surrounds this enterprise, including the idea, which was subsequently found to be false, that perfect specimens of the perfect race were specifically brought to these homes for the purposes of procreation. Though this, as I said, has been proved untrue, love, as we both know, defies exact definition. The love-act, as it is often referred to in an ambiguous use of words, is a complicated matter. We absorb what we can handle and no more. If we go too far the system breaks down. It is the belief of Klaus Mann, son of Thomas

Mann, that their home was so used. That too is disputed.

After the war my father refused to live in that house again. Heinrich and his wife Carlotta, however, felt differently and spent summers there. Carlotta wished for a system of greater security and decided to replace the gate. My brother's wife is immensely wealthy; security therefore is an obsession. I took the gate. I had it shipped here to open and close on to another landscape. Why? It seemed a symbolic gesture to me and quickly it seemed to me to be part of the new landscape of my life, Lake House. Which is strange because I took a number of other items also, which did not, it seemed to me, fit in. Perhaps we do not fully trust our memory, we need mementoes, and I was finished with that old house. And that is all. Your brother saw a gate that he associated with the heroic; your father saw a gift to make up for gifts he had not given; your mother saw that the gate was inappropriate, symbolic of what she did not wish to consider.

I suggest that you do not impart this information to your mother. It is unnecessary. I see her sometimes in the town. She is serene, I think. My remark that she resembled Harriet Calder, which I was aware at the time distressed you was, forgive me, inaccurate. Again, my apologies.

Perhaps we will see each other when you next return.

With affection,
Your friend,
Thomas

And I didn't tell her. I regretted asking him, really. Berated myself for asking for answers to long-ago questions, the answers to which would never provide balm for my wounds. In the end one must heal one's own. It's solitary work.

CHAPTER 19

She died suddenly. 'My mother died suddenly,' I say whenever anyone asks. Which is rarely, as you would expect. 'A coronary. Massive.' Or so he said, the doctor who rang me and I thought, but she's a small woman! 'Massive' seems wrong. I pulled the telephone off at the root and threw it against the wall. And I cried out 'No' and again 'No No'. And 'No'. But then everyone says no. And then the doctor rang my mobile. Which of course she'd given him. For emergencies. On my instructions. Mothers become more obedient as they grow older. And when he rang back I said, 'It's over,' and he remained silent. Like her. I went home for the funeral. A witness. The only family witness as it happens. Daragh, though he was not physically there, followed her out to where the others lay, walking beside me step by step. We must all find our own best way to endure.

Daragh did his mourning in another country. And I sent photographs of the graves. Helpful as ever. Bishop Fullerton said mass. He'd been 'very fond of Sissy O'Hara. Very fond.' Spoke to all of

222

us who'd come 'to see her off', which was virtually the entire town. Referred to the tragedy of 'Tom and Sissy's boy' and how she'd borne so much loss in 'her life of quiet courage and spiritual dignity here, in our community'. Lovely speech and then the letters! About what they'd meant, what she'd meant to everyone. How can I summarise? Or guide you to what lay beneath the weight of the words? Perhaps everyone knew that in a sense life had almost defeated them but they'd somehow loved on, loved life, had revered it still. I could tell from the letters that people seemed grateful to know that it is possible, that love can do that. Just in case. And if she'd shocked despair out of herself, once, years ago in a mental hospital, well, that's what was demanded to make the unendurable endurable. It was an honourable course. They'd lived close to what was lost. He'd always believed that was the only way.

And they had been happy. What more can one say?

CHAPTER 20

So time marched on without either of them. It's a quick-step. I relied on Patricia, Bridget's daughter, and on Bogus for stories of what was real, there, in the place that had become the dream-landscape of my life.

Once when I went back to deal with certain issues, as my solicitor put it, I visited Bogus. Aoife was resting so she couldn't greet me. The news was on. 'Gerry looks like a monk on TV, a real ascetic, don't you think Olivia? Martin doesn't, but is a very dedicated man. They're "naturals" on TV. Though Gerry's more natural than Martin. But I suppose Martin has other means of communication. And they know short and snappy works on television. Is it soundbites, they call them? You know, I think the newsmen seem a bit soft on them. Have we laden them down with guilt about Ireland, the sins of their fathers and grandfathers, their great-grandfathers? Ah now, here come the Unionists. Listen to them! Hopeless! Useless! Inarticulate! Apart from Paisley, who lacks a certain charm, wouldn't you say? Isn't it amazing, Olivia, they have no facility, none, in the language of the country to which they've sworn allegiance and for which they've often given their lives. No one understands their story, no one ever will, even if they knew how to tell it. What's the point? They've no history of oppression. And singing the praises of . . . King Billy? Oh for God's sake! The Battle of the Boyne? Oh dear, oh dear. And pride in a religion that, as they see it, had defeated Rome, the Mother Church. No one wants to defeat their mother. And no humour. None. At least if they'd sat beside Catholics they'd have got the rhythm of language and have learned how to tell a joke. They've had a poor education in the things that matter. Still, I suppose segregation means you won't be contaminated by another point of view. You know you're right, all the time, about every-thing. Both religions agreed on that, at least. They're together on the idea of segregation. It's a blessing. Do you not agree, Olivia? It's an educa-tion.' I couldn't answer because Aoife banged on the floor and he looked at me – with what? I'd rather not know. But he wrote it to me. Determined man, in his own way.

Forgive me, Olivia. I seem to be losing my way. Jim Brannigan's ill again. Marjorie may go to live in Dublin. Which I find a very painful thought. I'm sure, since you're a perceptive woman, that you've noted I'm not exactly impervious to the glories of

225

Marjorie Brannigan. 'Time cannot wither her', though it's withered me. Aoife is still not well. I do my best, Olivia, and I know it's a brutal thing to say but a permanently unwell wife breaks the spirit. A man must tell someone the secrets of his soul. Someone has to know. I want advice, Olivia. I've thought of writing Marjorie a letter. What do you think Olivia? Would a letter be a sin? A letter from me? It would, wouldn't it? I know. I'm prepared to lose my soul but I think it's lost already. It's hers. Marjorie has my soul. What can I do, what can my body, the temple of my soul, do but accompany it on its long, long journey of worship? If I had one hour with her after these decades of desire and waking dreams I would suffer the eternal flames of hell, laughing. I'd be laughing, as they say. There, my confession, Olivia, but I trust you more than any priest. Especially now.

Your friend,
Bogus

P.S. Does love drive you mad, Olivia? And now I have a terrible question. I keep asking myself this question, over and over. I keep thinking that if I get the answer right on this I'll have learned an essential thing. Ah, who am I to think that I could discover an essential thing? But my question, or is it our question, could it have been all for love? And sure isn't love just torture, Olivia! Was it love spirited Jean McConville away from her nine children? Men can be demons to women! Oh the long list of men and women loved to death for love of Ireland. I'll stop now. I'm tired and Aoife is calling me. Again. Burn this. I should never have written it – but I had to. I just had to. And I'll post it.

I wish he hadn't.

In our few other calls or meetings we made sure we were on safer ground. For us, at least. 'Hasn't the lexicon expanded through years, Olivia: broadcasting ban, the disappeared, human bombs, hunger strikes – didn't anyone warn that woman Thatcher of the significance of hunger strike in Ireland, didn't anyone mention the famine?' That, years later, became part of Holocaust Studies. Bridget, who feels very strongly about the Famine, goes to the theme-park – two hundred acres in Limerick – and, alas, she brings back photographs. And Bridget is not photogenic. Oh there's one I'd love you to see: she's standing beside a newly constructed coffin-ship, which I told her didn't seem to be her style at all. God – she looked daggers at me and sure I sent them winging back to her.

'She thinks her trump card is the granddaughter,

Carly – Carly Ní Houlihann – what are we coming to, Olivia? Eighteen now, at Trinity. "Brilliant girl" according to Bridget. French is her subject. Amazing when you think we're not exactly linguists. But maybe we are. I've heard Carly is living with her boyfriend, Eton boy, Tristan! Dresses like a tinker, but there you are. I suppose we've come a long way. Who ever thought the Taoiseach would be a separated man? Twice. Divorced? Well, as Bridget said, "it's complicated". Still, we've come a long way. Sexual intercourse – may I use that phrase, Olivia? It still shocks me to be able to say the words out loud – sexual intercourse began in Ireland rather later than 1963. But we caught up. I think we would both agree that we caught up. Much later, when we saw the light, when it came to light that the Bishop of Galway had an illegitimate son. "WHAT? NO!" Priests have no power over us any more.

'And once religion loses that power all that's left is love of God rather than fear of God. I suppose we've been more frightened in our bedrooms than we've . . . well, you know what I mean. Isn't He the ultimate Father? Who wants their father in the bedroom? Am I shocking you again Olivia? Why do I find it so easy to talk to you? We're great friends aren't we? Are you shocked? What's wrong with being shocked? Anyway, "Fuck 'em" is the feeling now. And fuck 'em we do. We're on "the long slide to happiness". Thanks for the Larkin, Olivia, though that long slide is a bumpier ride than people let on. Loved the last line of "I Remember, I Remember": "Nothing, like something, happens anywhere." We can't say that any more, can we, about Ireland? Have I gone too far, Olivia? Don't go now! Talk a bit more.' Though I hadn't said a word.

Bridget, as she grew older and felt perhaps that she did not have the time left to write a long letter about long ago, sent postcards. And annually, on St Patrick's Day, greetings for 'old times' sake', though no longer with a shamrock – 'It's not that fashionable any more. Only in America, for the parade.' And sometimes I saw her when I returned, which was rarely. She was careful with a woman from another tribe, as she saw me now. 'Ah Olivia, sure we'd hardly recognise you.' And then, 'Though I suppose it's because you're still the same!' Terrifying! She phoned occasionally. 'Mr Middlehoff has gone more into himself. Lost in himself. They say he's depressed. Ridiculous, I say. He's just sad. And of course he's got no religion. Nothing to help him. The sadness descended deep on him when Mrs Calder died a few months after his father. Though he was never a bundle of laughs, was he, Olivia? Now he doesn't want to talk to anyone, which in Ireland is a definite sign of insanity.' And she'd laugh. She was right, he probably was lost in himself. Lost in the old dream of Harriet Calder, talking to her silently, the way half the best conversations in a human life go on. Silently.

With ghosts. I wrote to him. His reply was short. The normal thank-you letter. A nothing thing really. Just manners.

The letters, the cards and the phone calls from Bridget and Patricia and Bogus grew less frequent as we moved inexorably towards that biblical moment, the millennium, when, with shock one realised one had lived much of one's life in another century. The last word on Robert Carter and Bishop Fullerton arrived without warning. Patricia was the messenger. She took time over it, news of death mustn't be rushed. Robert Carter died first. 'He always stayed loyal to Mr Middlehoff, Olivia. Perfidious Albion does friendship well,' she wrote. And I thought my mother would have laughed at that. I miss her laughter. Always will. Turned out Robert Carter was a war hero. He'd told no one, perhaps believing that an English war hero, even in the Ireland of the sixties and seventies, would not be welcome. Later perhaps he'd forgotten his heroism, sometimes people do, or perhaps he understood that a nation's history is like a carefully constructed family photograph album. There must be excisions. In fact the local paper, which Patricia sent to me, picked up the *Times* obituary and with great delicacy managed to explain in considerable detail the nature of his heroism, the courage with which he'd tended the wounded, without making much of the fact that he was an English soldier. It was a minor masterpiece of elective editing. Bishop Fullerton, who'd believed himself to be in the spiritual preservation business, a kind of area-manager for the Holy Father and for whom the Galway debacle had dealt a blow to his vision of Ireland as 'a unique gift to His Holiness, the ultimate example of the perfect Catholic country', was killed in a car crash on St Stephen's Day. He was driving himself. Eamonn was in the Caribbean on his Christmas holiday. 'The blessing of that!' Such a relief to Eamonn's family who'd long feared the death of a bishop on their conscience. The car belonged to the Palace and was a write-off. However Bishop Fullerton, knowing the car to be Palace property, left money to Eamonn to buy his family a new Mercedes. It came with the admonition to 'behold St Christopher! Then go thy way in safety, Eamonn, My Good Shepherd.' Which evidently had Eamonn's family in 'floods of tears, for days'. Tears that turned to laughter. The way tears do.

Though tears came again. We were crying for our friends, like everyone else that September day when the world changed. As did Ireland. And in the ashes of that September day in New York the Provisional IRA finally traced the outline of their own destruction. And that figure – over three thousand dead – became more than a question of mathematics. We'd started our own reckoning, over three thousand of our own dead, which in the context of Northern Ireland is the equivalent of six hundred thousand in America, and one hundred and fifty thousand in Britain. 'Quantity has a quality all its own,' as someone once wrote. Bogus rang me: 'It's over now, Olivia. Try raising money for the boys back home in a New York bar now.'

Bogus was right. Though we did not know it then, a discussion had been scheduled for 11 September 2001, between Mr Bush's representative, Mr Haass, and Gerry Adams concerning the 'Colombian Connection'. It was going to be very frosty anyway, but that day turned into one hell of a tough conversation as Americans fell from the sky and nine human bombers taught America what it was like to be blown to pieces for a cause. It was indeed over then. 'The boys' were nobody's heroes any more. And because they're fast learners they acted. Quickly. 'We're not like al-Qaeda.' That was a pretty important message to get across. And lo and behold, on 28 October 2001 the Army Council of the Provisional IRA declared that they had put all their weapons 'beyond use'. Forensic use of language. Even going back to 1923, when de Valéra called 'Time's up' during the Civil War, we 'buried' the weapons. And, unlike 'the disappeared', we remembered where we'd buried them. It was too important to forget. Arms, and the man who decides what to do with them, present a linguistic as well as a logistic challenge. It always has. After the disaster of the 1956–62 Border Campaign, Mr Ó Brádaigh ordered his men 'to dump arms', which is another thing altogether. Which everyone in Ireland knew, since careful interpretation is our forte. So 'weapons beyond use' was taken by many to be a statement of unusual clarity. We latched on to them, invested hope in them – hope that those three little words signified that the thirty-year war might begin to draw to a close. Though peace, we discovered, would be a long drawn-out affair.

Which was not true of the miracle, the absolute, irrefutable national miracle of Ireland, which turned out in the end to be economic. What a surprise the surprise ending to our sad story was. None could have guessed, none could have foretold that we would one day be one of the richest countries in Europe. This miracle did not come about as a result of a pilgrimage to Lourdes by tax inspectors and accountants. Oh no. Though the Hand of God must have been there, somewhere. Our increasing wealth, of which there was barely a hint in the eighties, became undeniable in the nineties. The Celtic Tiger settled down in a landscape that must have felt initially alien to him. Though he soon prowled his elegant path through the land, his progress noted by the whole world as he devoured every prejudice of those who'd ever, ever underestimated us. What a shock to them all! All we'd ever needed was a chance. That more or less summarised the feeling.

And it mattered in ways we could not imagine.

The present – now – was a very attractive place. More attractive than the past. 'Money, Olivia, is like a ticket to the future and at last we can afford the fare!'

Now that we had everything we could wait for the rest, for the dream. After all, who wouldn't want to join us when they could see just how great it was? Yes, we could wait for the North. We had the money now to wait it out. And we did. And in March 2007, one of the longest peace negotiations in modern history – thirteen years – drew to a close. It wasn't the moderates who won. Because during that time every decent and moderate politician had been sidelined in Northern Ireland and we were all left with the one 'who looked like a monk' and the one who'd taken Holy Orders all right, but not the ones with which we were familiar. Still we had peace. Of a kind. The exhausted hand of history had grabbed Gerry Adams and Dr Paisley, who, as Bogus wrote, were now 'ready for their close-up even though neither of them got what they wanted. And the world marvels at the smiles. Though no one, have you noticed, has run laughing into the streets. Might bump into the man or woman who murdered their brother or mother or maybe a cousin. That would spoil the whole thing. And they're given to a bit of strutting you know, Olivia, which might seem unforgivable, but after all they murdered for a noble cause. But I suppose peace is about forgiveness. No ASBO for them. I suppose it depends on what your definition of anti-social behaviour is.'

He was right. No one talked of victory marches. And it was all somehow low-key. After all that time and at the end of that long and bitter story we were only front-page news for a day. 'Thirty years of killing and in the end you sit down and talk.

'That's the lesson Olivia. Kill if you must but in the end you will have to talk. It's not the subject that matters. Remember that. It's the conversationalists. Who talks. That's what matters. But you know that already. Gerry certainly seemed happy. He smiled at the camera. He's used to smiling now. Starred in *VIP* magazine. Now that's not something one would have expected of Patrick Pearse or Wolfe Tone. Ian hadn't smiled much and who could be surprised at that? Martin McGuinness was thrilled. He can now get back to elucidating the virtues of education. He loves children and takes his responsibilities towards the education of the young very seriously indeed. Though the smiles were stunning the rhetoric was muted, I thought. Still, Gerry's take on it all was very positive. Ian Paisley's was positive. They were each of them positive. Which was great.

'But did you notice they were positive about different things? Entirely different things. And each of them was determined to write the last word. It's yes. Once Gerry said yes and accepted the Police Service of Northern Ireland. So it's yes all round. But say nothing yet. We all know that for the real last, last word you must wait.

'And bear in mind, Olivia, certain uncomfortable lessons are being learned by Gerry and Martin and Ian, lessons in realpolitik. And mark my words, Olivia, when Gerry comes marching down to Dublin and the South where all anyone is interested in is now and the future – well, the welcome won't be great. No. Gerry won't be hailed as the hero. Which will be a shock to him after all he'd done so much to bring the old dream closer? I'll give you a few reasons, Olivia and it won't matter what Gerry says. The bank robbery? God, Olivia, they looked stupid and then when they got the money they couldn't spend it. Now that's failure! Oh, the amnesia issue. Amnesia about Armagh. Which was clearly contagious, because when poor Robert McCartney was stabbed and sliced to death the seventy-two people who were there at the time, none of whom rang for an ambulance, simply couldn't remember a thing, not a thing. Isn't drink a demon? And even later, nothing came back to them, nothing. No matter how long those infuriating McCartney sisters persisted with their questions, all over the world meeting Presidents, Prime Ministers and even the Pope, trying to encourage someone to give "justice to our Robert". And we the land of memory and memories! Nothing came back. Blank. And I suppose the powers that be – always a mysterious group – thought, get those girls off the stage. We're in the middle of a Peace Process here.'

In May 2007 I was honoured to be invited – as a 'prominent Irish actress' – to the Taoiseach's address to both Houses of Parliament. The Prime Minister, Mr Blair, spoke first. He was optimistic, very positive about everything. Very generous. Paid proper tribute to John Major and Alfred Reynolds, John Hume and David Trimble. However, it seemed to me he made the conflict sound as though we'd had a minor tiff for about thirty years, which was strange considering he really had done so much to end it. Maybe he finds numbering the dead too painful a task. Mr Ahern – Bertie – was more grave, acknowledged the ghosts in the room. He paid tribute to Daniel O'Connell who'd built a mass civil rights movement and who'd died 160 years ago. But it was not, it seemed to me, the ghost of O'Connell who had brought us to this day. Other ghosts joined us and were acknowledged in that impressive hall. But as the litany of heroic sacrifice progressed the latest victims, who were perhaps only beginning to adjust to the eternal darkness into which they had been plunged, seemed folded, however unwillingly, into an ancient congregation. They were not named as they passed us by. For on that bright May day when our future shone before us we wished for neither their echo nor their shadow. Begone. We fare forward.

All in all, it was an historic moment. Which

everyone seems to be studying now. Everyone is learning our lessons. Slowly. And old soldiers leave the stage not necessarily in the time of their own choosing. Dr Paisley suddenly just slipped into the shadows and Bertie followed him: nothing terrible, slipstreams of life, I suppose, and love had at least something to do with it . . .

CHAPTER 21

It was late spring of the next year and I went to Ireland, 'one week, no longer, I promise', and was driving down to Wicklow with the radio on, which is unusual for me as I can never get the right station, when they announced Thomas Middlehoff's death. He must have been better-known than I'd realised, or maybe it was a poor day for news. I stopped the car and I rang Bridget. She was heartbroken. His family, his brother, was coming to take his body home to be buried in their family plot in Bavaria. 'Where he'd started from, I suppose. A nice man, Olivia. Very lonely. That woman! Couldn't forget her. My God, the day she died. Horrible. Years ago and I still can't forget it. The sounds he made! Frightening. I never told anyone. He was mad for weeks. Not screaming, oh no. Other sounds. Like I said, horrible. Love, Olivia, it's a terrible thing. That kind anyway. But I stayed. Faithful, I suppose I'm faithful by nature. I said to myself, "Pretend this never happened." I kept saying that to myself, "Bridget, pretend it never happened." And honestly, in time, it was like it hadn't happened at all.

239

We never referred to it. He was an abrupt man sometimes. But I grew very fond of him. He said I'd be looked after. As if I needed it! I'm a rich woman. I only worked for him a few days a week to keep me out of the house when I was divorced. Crazy what happened to Paddy and me. We were married for all those years, Olivia. And happy. I was left in my sixties for a girl in her forties. That seems to be the sum of it. What an old age he threw me into. Paddy isn't even happy with Finnoualla. At least Bogus will be happy with Marjorie Brannigan. Now that Jim's incarcerated she has a clear conscience. Well, reasonably. Better late than never. They'll have a few years together and I suppose everyone grabs what they can. A depressing thought, Olivia. I saw Brendan Begley's daughter the other day. She's off to Canada to join Brendan and Sorcha. Bitter pill for poor Mary who spent all this time bringing her up. God, that was a scandal when he upped sticks and left with Sorcha. A trained psychiatrist but couldn't run his own life. Are they happy, Brendan and Sorcha? Who knows. It's just a new fad, divorce in Ireland. Money brought it around. I'm beginning to think that's the reason. Love has nothing to do with it. We do it because we can afford to. Anyway, I'm a rich woman, Olivia. I've got my mother's house in Kilkenny. People commute from Kilkenny now. Did you know that? And I've got Granny's house down in Kerry. I rent it in the summer and it's worth a fortune. People crawl all over it in the summer. County Kerry, I mean. Yes. I'm rich. Mr Middlehoff may have been writing all that stuff about Ireland and our economic miracle but he still thought I was poor. Irish poor. Prejudice! Land! Land, Olivia. You were mad to sell your mother's house. Anyway, I've got to go now. Comfort yourself with the knowledge, Olivia, that at least a heart attack is quick. Like your mother.'

And I thought, too quick. And it must have been the shock but I started to cry, which upset Bridget.

'Now, now Olivia darling, it was the best way for her. And as for Mr Middlehoff, Olivia, his time was up. He was a very old man. I think his time was up the day Mrs Calder died. Yes, it was over then, for him. I know you're sad, very sad, Olivia. I know you liked him a lot.'

'I did,' I said.

And I thought to myself, I suppose I loved him, in the way that you love grace in your life. He was a graceful man. Who knew the battle. And knew that it's for ever. That there was no escape from love and loss and guilt. That it can't be helped. 'What can't be cured, love must be endured, love.' Yes, my father was right, Thomas Middlehoff was a man 'of a special understanding' who'd understood the event on that hot summer day when the sky rolled over us. And he understood how we'd cried out against it. And that it was to no avail. Oh how we'd cried out against it. Yes, he knew that. And above all he knew that however much one gets lost in the present, however much one

241

thinks the past has been obliterated, it comes back. It comes back to judge you. And you judge it, in the moral landscape of memory. Yes, he understood that the event, which had occurred in a small town in Ireland and had long been remembered by us all, had also been survived. But not without much difficulty.

BIBLIOGRAPHY

Benn, Gottfried (ed. Volkmar Sander), *Prose, Essays and Poems* (New York: Continuum, 1987)

Bew, Paul, *Ireland: The Politics of Enmity, 1789–2006* (Oxford: Oxford University Press, 2007)

Böll, Heinrich (trans. Leila Vennewitz), *Irish Journal* (New York: McGraw-Hill, 1971)

English, Richard, *Armed Struggle: The History of the IRA* (London: Pan, 2004)

Foster, R. F., *Luck and the Irish: A Brief History of Change, 1970–2000* (London: Allen Lane, 2007)

——, *Paddy and Mr Punch: Connections in Irish and English History* (London: Allen Lane, 1993)

——, *The Irish Story: Telling Tales and Making It Up in Ireland* (London: Allen Lane, 2001)

Grass, Günter (trans. Krishna Winston), *Crabwalk* (n.p.: Harvest Books, 2005)

——(trans. Michael Henri Heim), *Peeling the Onion* (London: Harvill Secker, 2007)

Hamburger, Michael and Christopher Middleton (eds), *Modern German Poetry 1910–1960* (New York: Grove Press, 1962)

Hull, Mark M., *Irish Secrets: German Espionage in

Wartime Ireland, 1939–1945 (Dublin: Irish Academic Press, 2004)

Moloney, Ed, *A Secret History of the IRA* (London: Allen Lane, 2002)

——, *Paisley: From Demagogue to Democrat?* (Dublin: Poolbeg Press, 2008)

Pearse, Patrick, *Plays, Poems and Stories* (Dublin: Phoenix Publishing Co., n.p.)

——, *Political Writings and Speeches* (Dublin: Phoenix Publishing Co., n.p.)

Reck-Malleczewen, Friedrich (trans. Paul Rubens), *Diary of a Man in Despair* (London: Macmillan, 1979)

Reich-Ranicki, Marcel (trans. Ewald Osers), *The Author of Himself: The Life of Marcel Reich-Ranicki* (London: Weidenfeld & Nicolson, 2001)

Schlink, Bernhard, *Heimat als Utopie* (Frankfurt: Suhrkamp, 2000)

Stern, Fritz, *Five Germanys I Have Known* (New York: Farrar, Straus & Giroux, 2006)

Sullivan, A. M., *Speeches from the Dock: Or, Protests of Irish Patriotism* (Dublin: H. M. Gill & Son, 1953)

Townshend, Charles, *Easter 1916: The Irish Rebellion* (London: Allen Lane, 2005)

Wellbery, David E. et al (eds), *A New History of German Literature* (Cambridge, MA: Belknap Press, 2004)